PRAISE FO[R]
STOLEN POSTCARDS

If you thrill at tiny wildflowers, single snowflakes, and that fleeting moment when the light is perfect—if you're likely to be at least as captivated by the little kid staring at the famous painting as you are the painting itself—then congratulations, for in Jan Ackerson's *Stolen Postcards* you have found a book you are sure to love.

— N. John Shore, Jr.
author, *Ashes to Asheville*

How Jan Ackerson can elicit genuine emotion from a reader in one hundred words is a gift of detail, language, and insight.

— Lisa Mikitarian
author and screenwriter/director, *SPENT*

Warning: These 100-word stories are as addicting as *Candy Crush*. Jan is a master wordsmith, creating mini-stories so emotive and vivid, you can't read just one.

— Theresa Santy
author, *On the Edge*

Jan Ackerson's gentle, lyrical voice gives us stories of everyday life that you will carry in your heart for weeks to come.

— Mimi Johnson
author, *Gathering String*

Someday I will master brevity as artfully as Jan Ackerson.

— Steve Buttry
veteran journalist and journalism professor

An extraordinary collection of powerful vignettes to make you laugh, cry, sympathize, and dream.

— Betty Castleberry
author, *Faylene in High Plains* series

In *Stolen Postcards*, Jan Ackerson, gifted author, presents humor, pathos, and memorable characters in short slices of real-life prose.

— Verna Mitchell
author, *Don't Frighten the Pansies*

STOLEN POSTCARDS

Jan Ackerson

BREATH OF FRESH AIR PRESS

Stolen Postcards

Copyright © 2016 Jan Ackerson
Published by Breath of Fresh Air Press

PO Box 12, St Clair NSW 2759
Australia
www.breathoffreshairpress.com.au

ISBN: 978-1-922135-39-1 (paperback)

National Library of Australia
Cataloguing-in-Publication Entry

Creator: Ackerson, Jan, author.
Title: Stolen postcards / Jan Ackerson
ISBN: 9781922135391 (paperback)
Subjects: Short stories.
Dewey Number: 823.92

Cover Photography: Pickrel Art & Photography, USA.
Cover Design: McClay Design, Canada.

DEDICATED TO

Ben

CONTENTS

INTRODUCTION

THERE'S AN ALMOST certainly apocryphal legend in which Hemingway claims he can write an entire novel in six words. The six words were "For sale. Baby shoes. Never worn." It is not important that Hemingway probably didn't write them. Someone did. And they powerfully prove the point. Sometimes a story is most beautifully told when it is rendered in the fewest words.

To grace brevity with beauty, however, requires an exacting mind, elegance in language, and depth of soul. The author of this book possesses these in abundance. Especially depth of soul, which you will soon enough discover for yourself.

Doug Worgul
Author of *Thin Blue Smoke* and *The Grand Barbecue*

JANUARY

ASHES

CICELY PONDERED THE ashes in the fireplace, working on a metaphor. It was almost too easy; they were cold, gray, dead. She'd use the metaphor to open a conversation she'd been working on for weeks. *John, I feel like these ashes are like our marriage...* She thought he'd appreciate the metaphor, if not the sentiment— he was a writer, after all.

John brushed by her shoulder. "'Scuse me," he said, kneeling. He blew on the ashes, once, twice. In moments, the fire crackled to life. He stood and took her hand. "Doesn't take long to start up again, does it?"

STUPID, STUPID

THE UNSEASONAL SUNSHINE belied my mood—I wished for the promised storms of the next day to complete my personal trifecta of guilt and self-loathing.

I've always been a fan of time travel fiction. Despite the grandfather-killing paradoxes, there's something appealing in the thought of going back in time to re-make that first impression, to undo that stupid act. But there would be no undoing what I had done. Stupid, stupid.

Still—I'd have given everything I owned for a time machine. Thoughts of *undo, undo* stole my sleep until early morning. I woke late.

The unseasonal sunshine belied my mood.

THE SECRET UNLEARNED

ELLIE GROPED THROUGH teenage hell, never discovering the secret of popularity. Strangely, she most envied the pretty girls' legs: slim, golden, with sharp and angular knees. Ellie's legs were stocky and white with rounded knees, and dots pinpointing every nub.

1

She tried to bestow popularity upon her daughters, but the secret of acceptable clothes and haircuts remained hidden. The girls, gifted with nonchalance, escaped unscathed.

Now Ellie is fifty, and a few lovely women have befriended her. She feels cloddish, unworthy—those secrets still elusive—and despite a lifetime of hearing that God sees only the inside ... it still matters.

J<small>ANUARY</small> 4

SHE RETURNED THE BAG

W<small>EARY FROM TRAVELING</small>, Krista tossed her roller bag onto her bed and flopped beside it, hoping to nap. But the bag was full of wrinkled and worn cut-offs and T-shirts, and Krista couldn't let it be. She sat up and unzipped the bag.

It was full of neatly folded, expensive clothing. Krista looked at the luggage tag; it belonged to a woman sixty miles away. There was a phone number, and Krista called it, wondering if the woman had made the same mistake, if she'd found Krista's dirty laundry.

She returned the bag—but she kept one pretty silk blouse.

J<small>ANUARY</small> 5

SLOW ... STOP

H<small>ANK HOLDS UP</small> one hand toward the woman in the Chrysler, then points to his sign. Just seconds ago, he'd flipped it from s<small>LOW</small> to s<small>TOP</small>. Now she'll have to wait while oncoming traffic clears the construction zone, and he can see her frustration.

Hank doesn't care; he feels great. When he came to work after yesterday's lesson at the library, something unnamable snapped into place. The most amazing thing—each letter in s-t-o-p and s-l-o-w, he realized, had *its own sound.*

He starts to spin the sign; the Chrysler lady, confused, inches forward. *Slow. Stop. Slow. Stop. Slow. Stop.*

J<small>ANUARY</small> 6

THE LAST MEAL

T<small>HE PLANE BUMPED</small> through mild turbulence, and Laura gripped her seat. Surely they were about to crash. She glanced at the nearby passengers; they were occupied with their iPads, their magazines. Many of them were sleeping.

Didn't they know they were about to die?

"Ma'am? Did you want chicken or pasta?" The flight attendant seemed oblivious to impending disaster.

I want a tender filet, medium rare. Steamed new asparagus swimming in butter. Fresh raspberries in cream. Good Lord, can't you feel that? We're going down!

"Ma'am?"

"The pasta, please." But when it came, she went straight for the gummy brownie.

CLEAN

KAYLA LIKES DOING laundry, unlike her neighbors who complain about the basement laundry room. The hard water dulls their clothes, and the dryers take three quarters for ten minutes of blistering air.

Kayla goes on Sunday mornings, when everyone is sleeping. She uses the hottest water possible for her tiny, soiled garments, and she leans against the cool concrete blocks while the machines agitate.

The best part is when she pulls items from the dryer, almost too hot to touch. She folds them into small stacks, pausing occasionally to hold a garment against her cheek. She feels clean, clean, clean.

ANOTHER NINETY DOLLAR SCARF

THE SCARVES WERE beautiful—one a swirl of tangerine and pink, the other a deep blue paisley. Melanie let one slip between her fingers, the silk so fine she could barely feel it. She pictured her overflowing closet, imagining outfits that would be perfect for each scarf, and she couldn't decide.

Holding the paisley to her throat, Melanie thought: *they're so expensive. I really don't need another ninety dollar scarf. I could easily donate that money to charity.*

With a nod, she left the store without making a purchase. The tangerine and pink scarf felt like nothing in her pocket

SUCH HORRIBLE SUFFERING

PATSY SEES THE lump on the road from far away, and the words *dead possum* flit through her consciousness. But as she gets closer, she sees that it's not *dead,* it's simply *wounded*. The unfortunate animal is ineffectually scrambling with its back legs. Briefly and ridiculously, Patsy considers taking it to a vet.

The animal haunts her thoughts all day. *Such horrible suffering.*

After work, she flicks on the television, eager to forget. *I hope it wasn't in pain.* When the commercial comes on—the one with the wide-eyed brown children—she changes the channel, with a grunt of irritation.

JANUARY 10

SHE HATED DRIVING

MARTIN SOMETIMES FELT Val married him just to drive her around. She *hated* driving.

"C'mon, what's the worst that could happen?"

Val thought about it. "It's a stormy night. I'm lost. There's a warning light on, and the gas is on 'empty'. I feel diarrhea coming on. A tire blows out, and a strange face appears at the window. *That* could happen."

When Martin was gone for a week, Val figured she'd just walk, or stay inside.

"Come visit me!" said her daughter. "We'll have a blast!"

Val wanted to go, but she looked outside—cloudy. "I can't," she said.

JANUARY 11

BLESSINGS

THE VOICE ON the radio mesmerizes Tilda. "You cannot expect to reap a harvest of prosperity, children, if you do not sow *all* of your seed!"

Tilda leans in closer.

"Do you want blessings?" Tilda nods. "Give everything you own to obtain them!"

Tilda has already sold her home; she sent a large check to the radio voice the very day of her closing. She lives now in a tiny apartment, far from her children and grandchildren.

The voice continues, and she settles her gaze on a jewelry box. She'll sell them tomorrow—surely *then* the promised blessing will come.

JANUARY 12

WHISPERS AND LAUGHTER

GWENDOLYN STRUGGLES TO get out of her car at the supermarket parking lot, and perspiration dots her forehead. It's not far to the doors, but she wheezes hard for a few seconds after squeezing into a scooter.

Once inside, she can hear the whispers and laughter, and when she maneuvers her scooter past a teenage boy, he makes piggy noises. She sets her jaw and looks straight ahead, humming a melody from a musical.

At home, she sinks into a chair. A tiny kitten hops up and kneads her enormous bosom with its paws, purring its way into her soul.

JANUARY 13

FIFTEEN BLOCKS

THE GALLERY OPENING was fifteen blocks away, but Fiona decided to walk. The fresh air would do her good.

At the first intersection, she was joined by several people, dressed for the same occasion. The light said DON'T WALK, and Fiona waited obediently while the others strolled past her, after a perfunctory check for traffic. A woman looked back at her, smiling.

A disaster waiting to happen, she thought, lips pressed together. *They should wait for the light.*

Fourteen blocks later, the scenario having repeated fourteen times, Fiona finally got to the party. It had started long ago, without her.

JANUARY 14—ORGANIZE YOUR HOME DAY

TO-DO LIST

BETTE, WHAT'S THIS?

Oh, that's my 'to-do' list for today. I'm loving retirement—so much more time to do chores.

'Iron drapes?'

They've needed ironing forever.

'Alphabetize spices?'

I couldn't find the cumin yesterday.

'Scrub grout in upstairs bathroom?'

Have you seen *the upstairs bathroom?*

So ... how'd it go?

I started on the spices. We've got three cumins. That amused me, so I blogged about it.

And the curtains? The grout?

Who irons curtains? And I'll do the bathroom next time Marcy visits.

So ... you found cumins, and wrote in your blog.

Yep. It was a busy day. I'm exhausted.

ONE TEAPOT SHORT

DORA LEFT LATE, flustered at having to search for her keys. She meant to visit the library, but frustration sent her to the emporium. She clenched her jaw and massaged her temples.

At the market, she examined a whimsical teapot. *It's perfect for my collection.*

Defiantly, she carried the teapot into her house. Stepping carefully inside, she pushed back a box of newspapers, searching for a spot for the teapot. A shelf on the far wall looked promising; Dora navigated a maze of trash, then shifted several items to make room.

The house sighed, just one teapot short of bursting.

TWO GLASSES

ONE HELD A beautiful, amber liquid, and Lily knew that it would slip warmly down her throat, whispering *hello, friend.* The other fizzed and bubbled with innocence. Lily hadn't tasted innocence in years; she wondered if it would whisper to her, and if she would still recognize the language.

Two glasses. Lily rested her forehead in her hands and imagined that first golden sip.

She could hear the hiss of a thousand tiny bubbles in the second glass, and she watched as the ice gently settled.

Two glasses. With trembling fingers, Lily reached out and took a drink.

THE BEST LIFE

WHEN CORNELIA NOTICED a forgotten purse in the lecture hall, she took it, fully intending to contact its owner. But first, she thought, she'd play a little game. She spilled it onto her table, feeling slightly thrilled.

A Guerlain lipstick—*Provocative*

A photograph of a fat puppy

A ticket for an Adele concert

A receipt: two blouses, size 4

This woman has the best life. She took the billfold, found an address. Eighteen miles—she drove to the woman's house and returned the purse to its grateful owner.

As she left, she ineffectually kicked the wheel of the woman's Lexus.

NEAT BLOCK LETTERS

TODAY WILL BE the day.

She finds her favorite pen—a ballpoint, but not a gel. She dislikes gel pens; her left hand smears them as she writes. And she loves the scratch of a ballpoint pen on newsprint.

Her dilemma is this: although she prefers to work the daily crossword in pen, she can't bear to make a mistake—inerasable, blotchy.

1 across: *Scandinavian currency*

KRONA, she writes, in neat block letters.

Several words later, it becomes obvious that the word was supposed to be KRONE. She crumples the puzzle and tosses it into the bin, her throat tight.

FACEBOOK MEME

I DON'T USUALLY do these things, but Donna tagged me, so … What do you regret?

1. Everything I've ever cooked with margarine, canned soup, or Velveeta.
2. That perm in the 70s, and my tall bangs in the 80s.
3. Not telling him I love him often enough. Not SHOWING him.
4. Toe socks. Head bands. Leg warmers.
5. High school. Everything about high school.
6. The hamster was a colossal mistake. Hamsters don't love you, and they stink.
7. Reading *Jonathan Livingston Seagull*. Thinking it was profound.
8. Thunking my son on the head in anger when he was only five.
9. Unkind words.
10. Unkind words.
11. Unkind words.

THE END OF THE SEASON

SEVENTEEN WEDDINGS IN twelve weeks—Thad was glad wedding season was nearly over. He cued the Macarena, then tilted back in his chair and rested his head on the wall. The guests performed the silly moves in their cocktail dresses, and Thad thought it ironic that he worked in an industry that glorified eternal love, when love had never presented itself to him.

When the song ended, Thad played a slow dance. He bent down to untangle a coil of cable when his eyes were drawn to the pretty photographer's assistant, sitting alone and eating a plate of rubber chicken.

SUFFOCATING

VANESSA IS NOT a hugger. A hug makes her feel as if she is suffocating, and her heart skitters into her stomach. When people approach her with a hug apparent in their attitude, Vanessa gives them the stiff arm.

Thom has just asked her to marry him. He is an endearing cliché on one bent knee, brandishing a little velvet box, his eyes sparkling and eager. Vanessa would like nothing more than to marry this goofy man.

But *yes* is caught in her throat. She is visualizing a receiving line and wondering if she could endure that—even for Thom.

DETOUR

ANNE WAS LATE for the dentist, but where she wanted to turn right, a DETOUR sign directed her straight ahead. Her pulse quickened. She only knew one route, and the orange signs were leading her into unfamiliar territory.

Finally, the detour ended. Anne took the first right, into a neighborhood where streets curved in unpredictable directions. Her armpits itched. She checked the time. Twelve minutes late.

When at last she found a main thoroughfare, she pulled into a parking lot and started to call the dentist. Then she saw where she was—and went in to get a doughnut, instead.

ONE-WAY TICKET

THE GAL AT the ticket counter was checking her phone for messages when Dee walked up, wanting to buy a ticket. "Where to, ma'am?" she said.

"Duluth. I'm going to Duluth, Minnesota."

"Round trip?"

"No." Dee cleared her throat, then said it a second time, louder. "No, I want a one-way ticket, please."

Who buys a one-way ticket to Minnesota? thought the ticket agent. *Poor lady. Homely, too.*

She didn't see that Dee was bouncing on the balls of her feet, or the pulse that beat rapidly in her throat. She didn't see the bundle of letters in her purse.

CLOWN COLLEGE

MRS. PORTERFIELD STUDIED Andrew's transcript. "Your grades are excellent. What colleges are you considering?"

Andrew grinned. "I want to go to clown college."

She peered at him, speechless.

"I want to make people laugh. Everybody likes to laugh, right?"

She tried to remember laughter. "I can't allow you to—"

He stood, and with a flourish, produced a bouquet of silk flowers from his sleeve. Mrs. Porterfield pushed them away, but Andrew gave an exaggerated sneeze, then fell backward onto a Whoopee cushion.

Unbidden, laughter pushed past the barriers in Mrs. Porterfield's heart and out of her nose, the tiniest squeak.

MAYBE

MAYBE TODAY IS the day that I'll step out on the porch, then keep walking all the way to the sidewalk. Maybe my rebel heart won't pound so hard that my breath retreats. Maybe I'll feel a breeze on the tiny hairs of my arms, and not feel alarmed that the world is too near.

Maybe today is the day that I'll walk a few short blocks for a candy bar. Maybe I'll remember what it is to have warm sun at the nape of my neck. Maybe I won't feel the fingers of panic strangling me, instead.

Maybe tomorrow.

A FIT OF WHIMSY

WHEN THE ELEVATOR doors opened, one of the festively-dressed people said, "Going to the reception?"

Rhoda considered her business suit, her sensible shoes, and was overcome by a fit of whimsy.

"Yes!" she said, and rode with them to the atrium.

Obviously there was no place card for her, but she worked the room. To the bride's friends, she was the groom's British cousin. To the groom's friends, she was the bride's friend from Sydney. Her accents were entirely unconvincing. She danced and danced.

Later, her husband called. "How's the conference?" he said.

"Borrrrrring," she said. She burped, tasting champagne.

JANUARY 27

BETWEEN OATMEAL AND GRANOLA

AMBER WAS ALMOST done shopping when she realized she didn't need jelly, after all. But the jelly aisle was on the other side of the store, and Amber was tired. She looked over her shoulder—no one was watching—then set the jar on a shelf, between oatmeal and granola.

At home, Amber couldn't stop thinking about the jelly. She wondered if putting it on the wrong shelf was a sin. Someone would have to reshelf the jar, after all, and maybe they'd be angry. Maybe they'd even curse.

She added the jelly to her already heavy burden of guilt.

JANUARY 28

THE THIRTIETH TABLET

A SPIDER SPRINTED across Sonya's sink just as she was opening her pill bottle. She was damp from her shower, not even dressed, and she yelped, throwing her hands up and scattering the pills.

She knew exactly how many there were—the bottle was new. She searched the bathroom, muttering, but only found 29 tablets. Worried about the sniffy dog, she closed the bathroom door as she left for the market, the library, the bank.

Back home, she headed for the mirror to comb her breeze-blown hair. There was the tablet, glued to her cheek, like some fluorescent yellow wart.

JANUARY 29—PUZZLE DAY

JIGSAW PUZZLE

LES SHOOK HARRIET's hand, then looked over her shoulder. "Hey, is that a jigsaw puzzle?" He pushed into the room to where she was working on a 1500-piece lighthouse.

Harriet cursed her sister for this matchmaking attempt and followed Les to the table. He was picking up pieces, trying them here and there, setting them back in random places.

"Oh, don't—" she said. She went into the kitchen and made tea.

By the time he left, Les had completed the red lighthouse roof. Harriet watched him go, then hastily disassembled the roof, along with most of the sky around it.

JANUARY 30

MORE BEAUTIFUL

THE ARTIST'S UNHAPPY bare feet discovered the shattered pot on the floor. Eleven large chunks, four smaller ones; the rest was dust. He didn't need this pot, but he realized he was reluctant to discard it. Carefully, he turned the pieces, looking for places where the jagged edges matched. Satisfied that enough of the pot remained to reassemble, the artist looked toward his workshop shelves for the right material for the job. His eyes fell on two little containers, side-by-side. Lacquer—and why not? Flakes of gold. *Kintsukuroi:* a vessel that is far more beautiful—because it has been broken.

JANUARY 31

SATISFYING

THERE ARE TWO paths open to Kelly, and she has no idea which one to take.

During the day, she works in a homeless shelter as a candidate nun. She has picked lice from the heads of dozens of children, has clasped the hands of weeping women, painfully thankful for the small basket of toiletries and the bowl of soup.

At night, she can be found in an underground boxing club. She dances at the ropes, shakes sweat from spiked hair. She has never felt happier than the time her fist connected with her opponent's nose with a satisfying *crunch*.

FEBRUARY

SENSIBLE ONLY TO HER

THE MILLBURY PUBLIC Library consisted of 537 volumes, previously the property of Harold Pershing. Now his daughter Margaret maintained the shelves, with an organizational system sensible only to her.

Cam Willmore walked in, holding an index card. Margaret squinted darkly at his cap; he removed it and asked, "Got any books by ..." He showed her the card. "... Dumas?" He pronounced it *dumb ass*.

"No," said Margaret. "I do not."

He scanned the shelf behind her. "You sure?"

"Good day, Mr. Willmore."

After he left, she walked to a shelf and lovingly caressed the spine of *The Count of Monte Cristo*.

MOTIVATIONAL SPEAKER

A WOMAN IN a coral suit paced the stage, gesturing expansively, occasionally adjusting her wireless microphone. Background music ebbed and swelled in concert with her words; a slideshow of inspirational images played behind her. For an hour, she exhorted her avid listeners to put aside their regret, and she left them with this clever acronym:

Releasing
Everything
Grievous
Really
Enables
Transformation

After the seminar, Theresa got into her car, mumbling. *The biggest thing I regret is this stupid workshop. How'm I supposed to release that, huh? Are you going to transform my two thousand bucks back into cash for me.*

DOODLE

THE WORST THING about teaching is attending interminable workshops and seminars designed to improve my teaching. In reality, they improve nothing, but they take me away from my students, who always take advantage of the hapless substitute.

I sit in the back this time so I can doodle while the humorless presenter drones on, waving her pointer at text-heavy PowerPoint slides.

Finally free, I make a beeline for the parking lot, when a voice behind me calls out. "Hey," she says. "You dropped this."

Not my doodle.

She grins. "I've seen worse. Last week, some guy drew me with horns."

FRAGILE, PERISHABLE

A LETTER ARRIVES every day for a year, and Kellie saves them all, unopened, until the box is too full. She tapes it up, writes a familiar address on it, and takes it to the post office.

"Is there anything liquid, fragile, perishable, or dangerous in here?" asks the clerk. Kellie shakes her head.

"Anything valuable? Do you want it insured?"

"No," says Kellie. "It's not valuable." She pays $5.47 and drives home.

Two weeks later, the letters finally stop coming. Kellie watches the postman leave, resisting the urge to run after him. *Don't you have a letter for me?*

A NEW WEATHER TERM

LAUREN LEARNED AN unfamiliar weather term on her way to work. She'd never heard of 'Apache fog' before, but when the weathercaster mentioned it, she nodded; it *was* hard to see through the thick, low mist.

It was a good thing, though—because it gave her the inspiration she'd been needing. That evening, excited, she told Dave the name for her novel-in-progress. "Apache Fog! Isn't it great?"

"What does it mean?"

"I'm not sure—I heard it on the way to work. Like Indian summer, maybe?"

"Lauren … it's a patchy fog. *Patchy.*"

She squinted, sighed, walked out of the room.

FEBRUARY 6

BRAID

KATRINA HADN'T CUT her hair in decades. It took hours to wash and braid it, and it stayed damp for days. When she sat, lifting her huge braid to rest on a chair, a lightness traveled from her scalp into her chest.

Her children have finally persuaded Katrina to cut it, and she leaves the salon holding her daughter's hand, carrying the braid in a canvas bag. She feels dizzy, untethered.

At night, she feels as if her head might float off the pillow. Sleep won't come until she fetches the bag and drapes the severed braid around her shoulders.

FEBRUARY 7

NEW NEIGHBORS

DON LOOKED OUT the window, then turned to Natalie in disgust. "I don't like them living next to us. I don't want you to have anything to do with them, you hear me?"

"Yes, dear," Natalie said. Truth be told, they made her nervous, too. She didn't understand their sibilant language, their discordant music, the exotic smells of their food.

But when Natalie was hanging her laundry, the woman next door met her eye, wiggled her fingertips, shyly smiled. Natalie looked away, hoping Don hadn't seen. She thought how pretty was the woman's complicated dress, exactly the color of marigolds.

FEBRUARY 8

NOT TODAY, BUT NEXT WEEK

IF THINGS CONTINUE like this, I'll be on the streets soon. Melinda wondered what else she could do without. She'd given up cable, started walking to work. She ate once a day.

That day, when training a new cashier, Melinda saw how many errors Kimberly made. How easy it would be to slip a few twenties from her drawer … not today, but next week, when the dim girl was on her own. Kimberly's drawer would come up short, and she'd be reprimanded. Nobody would suspect Melinda. *So easy …*

She watched Kimberly struggle with change for $5.17 and made her decision.

SIX MONTHS AS A …

YVONNE PARKER'S NONFICTION series *Six Months as a …* was a huge bestseller. She'd spent half a year as a Luddite, a blackjack dealer, a line cook, a tuba student.

Her most recent book—*Six Months as a Soap Opera Addict*—was by far the most successful, and Yvonne just completed a national tour. The tone of her media blitz was mocking condescension.

Now she is working on *Six Months as a Dog Walker*. Every evening, she spends a few minutes assembling baggies and treats for the next day—all the while, she's thinking, *I wonder what Rodrigo is doing now.*

A LOGICAL MAN

HE WAS SUCH a *logical* man.

"You know how the show ends, right?" he said. "We'll leave before the last number, beat the jam at the parking lot."

She nodded, sighed.

"The restaurants are packed on Valentine's Day," he told her. "Let's go out on the 10th. It'll be more relaxed." She ordered salmon and tiramisu on the 10th, and four days later, she made meatloaf at home, a lump in her throat.

That evening, feeling peevish, she watched his freckled hands as he opened a jar of apricots, and as he scratched the dog's ear. *My sweetheart,* she thought.

AT THE DMV

MARLENE TOOK NUMBER 58 when she entered the DMV. A clerk called, "Number 26?" and Marlene snorted with exasperation. She strode to the counter, waving her number.

"I can't wait forever!" she said. She took out an official-looking badge. "Do you know who I am?"

"No, ma'am," said the clerk. She looked around Marlene and beckoned to Number 26.

Marlene stomped to a chair, sighing dramatically.

Someone tapped on her shoulder. Marlene turned to see an old man, tooth-less and malodorous. She recoiled, but he held out his hand, with the number 29 tab. "I don' mind waitin'," he said.

ON THE BUS

ROBERT NEVER RIDES the bus—but he did that day.

Robert never notices scents—but he did that day. She sat in front of him, smelling of wildflowers.

Robert never sees details—but he did that day, two small freckles on her left shoulder.

Robert never speaks to strange women, and although he planned to follow her (he imagined tipping his hat, holding a door), he stayed in his seat, blushing.

He knows it would be foolish to take the bus again in hopes of seeing her. Still, once a year he rides downtown, holding his cane between his knees.

KISS

DENISE WAS FETCHING a spoon for her hostess when the lights went out. She thought about finding a flashlight, but this was not her kitchen. In the next room, the guests laughed about the unexpected darkness.

She was feeling her way toward the door when she bumped into someone. "There you are!" said a voice she vaguely recognized. "Sorry I dragged you here, honey," he said, and he pulled her close, kissed her sweetly.

Denise knew this man would be horrified if he knew she was not his *honey*. Nevertheless, she relaxed into the kiss, hoping the darkness would stay.

NOT A FIDDLE

MAMA MARRIED BENEATH her station. I didn't understand that when I was little, even asked her once could we go to her station. When I was older, I understood. "I married for love, Janey," she told me.

"Mama," I said once, "who's this old feller holdin' a fiddle?" I showed her an old photograph I'd found.

"That's a violin," she said, "and that's your great-grandfather. He played beautifully."

"But could he play like Daddy?"

"No, Janey. No one plays like your daddy."

Daddy went to her, swung her around the kitchen, and kissed her till I decided to run outside.

IN THE WRONG PLACE

EDITH SAT TO rest in Jurassic Hall, amid dusty animatronic dinosaurs emitting recorded roars. On the next bench, a little boy of six or seven was talking to his mother, clearly agitated. "Triceratops was a *Cretaceous* dinosaur. It's in the wrong *place.*"

While the boy's mother tried to reason with him (*The scientists just might know more than you do, Phillip*), Edith remembered another little boy with a plastic dinosaur in each hand. He could barely talk, but he could name every creature. Edith fondly recalled his *thtegothauruth.* She had it still, in the same drawer as the winter gloves.

MATCHING

JENNY ADORES WEARING mother-daughter outfits with Eloise. She created the first outfit serendipitously—tiny jeans and a pink tee for Eloise were easy enough to reproduce from Jenny's closet. Since then, she's looked online for truly matching outfits. There were purple gingham sundresses when Eloise was two, and a precious cowgirl outfit when she was three.

Today's outfit is the cutest: pleated black miniskirt, Hello Kitty tank top. Best of all: Jenny bought it as a surprise. Imagine Eloise's face when she comes home from high school to see her mother in the very same outfit. Won't she be … delighted?

MOST PROMISING

WHEN SHE GRADUATED from high school, Annalise got the award for 'Most Promising Artist'.

In community college, her instructor praised her 'economy of line' and featured her work in a showcase of top students.

She waited tables for a year, spent three months visiting museums in France and Italy, then came home to paint.

"Can I really do this, Mama?" she said.

Her mother fumbled sadly with her thin wedding band. "Sweetheart, you can do anything you set your mind to."

Now, every so often, she slips into her small second bedroom and sits quietly amid stacks of unfinished canvasses.

NO STITCHES NEEDED

DR. RICHMAN EXAMINED the gash on Emma's forehead while Emma whimpered, clearly frightened. "Shhhh," he said, patting her hand. He turned to Cecilia. "How did this happen?"

"I'm so sorry! I just looked away for a second, and she's a wobbly walker, and I'm alone at home ... she fell and hit her head on the bookshelf."

Emma was whimpering louder now.

"Well, you're lucky. She won't need stitches. Don't kick yourself, please. This happens all the time." He hesitated, then scrawled a number on a prescription pad.

"Alzheimer's patients can be stressful. Call me—anytime—if you need to talk."

LEXIE'S TEACHABLE MOMENT

LEXIE HELD UP her chicken nugget. "Hey, Mom," she said. "Know what's funny?"

"What?"

"Chicken nuggets and chicken on the farm. Same *word*."

Joy bit her lip. "Honey, that's because ... you're *eating* a chicken."

Lexie dropped the nugget, eyes wide. She thought for a moment. "Is there a hamburger animal?"

"Hamburger is a cow, honey." Joy watched her daughter for signs of trauma.

"All cut up?"

"Yep."

"What about bacon?"

"Pig."

Lexie considered this. "Is there a French fry animal?"

"No, sweetheart," said Joy. "That's just potatoes."

Lexie picked up two nuggets, studied them, grinned. "*Bawwwk*," she said. "*Bawwwk, bawwwk!*"

HAUNTED

WHEN AIMEE WAS little, she thought her mother was haunted by a gray ghost. On haunted days, her mother moved little and spoke less. Her eyes sank into her skull, and she gave Aimee odd, thoughtless meals like sour pickles and apple-sauce.

Aimee could tell when the gray ghost was nearby; on those days, her mother was snappish, and Aimee retreated to her room.

Now she is grown up, on her own. The gray ghost moved into her apartment last week, but Aimee was not surprised. She'd been feeling peeved for days. She welcomed the ghost like an old friend.

FIGHT ON

I WROTE MY first song about my brother, who died of leukemia at twelve. In my song, Toby is determined to fight until his sword and shield are taken away. It got a million hits on YouTube, and now everyone knows me, the girl with the dead brother.

Except Toby wasn't that kid. He yelled and swore and smacked the nurses' hands.

My parents spent three years pushing me away; it's when I discovered guitar.

The whole world knows noble Toby now, and even Mom and Dad believe in that version of their little son. Time to write another song.

AT THE MAYFIELD INN

WHEN SERENA AND her friends checked into the Mayfield Inn, Serena was last to get a room key.

"We're switching to electronic keys," the clerk said. "Your room isn't done yet, sorry." She gave Serena an old-fashioned brass key.

The room was quaint—no television or telephone. No electric outlets. She changed and headed out to meet the girls.

"Isn't this great?" she said. "I don't even miss electricity."

The girls were puzzled; their rooms were fully modern.

When Serena went back to her room, she looked outside. Horses and buggies, gas streetlamps. And no way to open the window.

FEBRUARY 23 — PLAY MORE CARDS DAY

SOLITAIRE

WITH ONLY THREE aces played, and every pile with a club at the end, Kari knew the game of solitaire was lost. She flipped through the cards remaining in her hand, but there were no more plays. The ace was probably under the far right pile — yes, there it was. Kari pulled it out and played it alongside the other aces. The rest of the cards fell neatly into place.

"I can't believe you did that," said Joel. "How satisfying is it to win a game when you've cheated?"

Kari examined her conscience. Yep, totally satisfying. She dealt another hand.

FEBRUARY 24

DISGUSTING

THE CHUBBY WOMAN in front of me is scanning a tabloid while she waits to unload her grocery cart. I look at what has grabbed her attention.

TWO-HEADED CAT GIVES BIRTH TO SIX-LEGGED KITTEN!

From the items in her cart — mostly junk food — I can tell she's going to buy the tabloid. Sure enough, she tosses it between the pork rinds and the popsicles.

I would never allow such disgusting things to enter my body. My body is a temple. I clear my throat a little, hoping she'll look back at me and see what a healthy person looks like.

FEBRUARY 25

TOMORROW, A FAMILY CRISIS

THE PHONE RANG just as Toni was tying her running shoes. It was Bev, with a question about their favorite television show that led to a political discussion and a rant about the price of gas. An hour later, Toni changed into jeans — too late for a run today.

The next morning, Bev called again. So sorry, but could she stop by with something important?

Toni looked at the clock and shrugged.

The *something* turned out to be a pan of double-chocolate brownies. Irresistible.

When Bev left considerably later with an empty pan, she stood on Toni's porch and grinned.

UNRESPONSIVE TO THERAPY

THEY FOUND HER wandering the street in the small hours of the night. She was dressed in rags, missing one shoe. Clearly confused, she wept and muttered.

"No identification?" asked the police sergeant.

"Nothing. Says her name's Ella. No last name. Doesn't seem to be drunk or high. Just … off."

They sent her to the mental facility; she stayed for a long time. Dr. Prince was her therapist, and he marveled at the consistency of her delusions. *Pumpkins, mice, glass slippers … what a shame she's unresponsive to therapy. Deep-rooted trauma in her past, no doubt. Such a lovely, lovely girl.*

IN THE SUBWAY

DEBORAH READ, HER head down, while the subway clacked through its stations. She was aware of the man sitting heavily next to her, but she inched toward the window and dug in with her shoulder.

When the train sped through a tunnel, Deborah sighed and moved her thigh away from the man's jeans.

The train screeched to a halt, still in the tunnel; the only light came from a flickering tube overhead. Deborah's panicked breath stalled in her throat. When she made a choking sound, the man said, in a surprisingly childlike voice, "Ma'am? Would you hold my hand, please?"

A WRINKLE IN THE CARPET

BEAU'S AUNT NORA is a businesswoman. She was at a conference during our wedding, but when work brought her to town, we invited her for lunch. And then Beau called: running late, could I deal with her myself?

When I answered her knock and reached out to shake her hand, she pulled her purse close and looked past my shoulder into the living room. She sniffed.

"Come in, Aunt Nora," I said. "Please—have a seat."

She walked to a chair and brushed it off, then perched on the edge. Her lips curled, more of a sneer than a smile.

"Nora, would you like a cup of tea while the quiche finishes baking?"

When I brought the teacup, she nodded toward the end table. She didn't touch it.

I stammered through some small talk. After a few awkward moments, Aunt Nora stood.

"I've just now remembered an appointment. Give my best to Beau."

She walked toward the door; her shoe snagged a wrinkle in the carpet and she stumbled. I reached out to steady her, my hand grasping her elbow. Nora's face flashed repulsion; she brushed my mocha hand from her porcelain arm and murmured *thank you* from clenched jaws.

MARCH

BENEFICIARIES

LYNNE LISTENS TO her mother's lawyer as he read off the beneficiaries of her will—mostly children's charities and oddly, a parrot refuge. Lynne nods; she'd known for years that her mother collected charities. It's fine, it really is. Lynne doesn't really need the money, and she's happy on behalf of the needy children. She's even happy, she supposes, for the parrots.

Still, she's astonished when the lawyer shows her the final number, with all those digits. She remembers a lifetime of birthday presents scrounged from flea markets and rummage sales: a rusty lunchbox, an incomplete puzzle, that despicable doll.

SIXTIETH ANNIVERSARY

FOR THEIR SIXTIETH anniversary, Bertha and Lyle decided to fly somewhere. Neither had ever flown, but their delighted daughter booked their flight, their hotel, theater tickets.

At the airport, Bertha was distressed when they took her big shampoo bottle, and Lyle cursed at the overly-familiar TSA officer.

"It'll be an easy connection!" Louise had said, but Bertha and Lyle wandered around the second airport for hours. They had coffee and muffins, outrageously priced, then went to the wrong gate. They didn't hear their names being paged.

They missed their flight and took a long bus ride home, enjoying the scenery.

CONFESSION

I DESTROYED HER book; I admit it.

She reads it every evening, then sets it on the coffee table. I wish she paid more attention to me. I thought if I just moved the book—hid it, maybe—she'd

23

look around, see me looking at her, and we could have some time together. She knows I adore her. She *should* know.

Nevertheless, I didn't intend to destroy it. I only wanted to get the distraction out of the room. But one thing led to another...

If I look sad at her and wag my tail, she'll forgive me, I hope.

MARCH 4—NATIONAL GRAMMAR DAY

POSSESSION

RUTHIE REALLY COULDN'T stand it anymore. She passed the *Paw's and Claw's* sign daily on her morning walk, and finally she had to say something.

The woman behind the desk looked up and smiled. "Can I help you?"

Ruthie pointed at the window. "I just wanted to tell you—you shouldn't put an apostrophe on a plural. You don't need one on 'paws' or 'claws.' Apostrophes indicate possession. I thought you'd like to know."

"Thanks," said the woman. "I'll get right on that. Oh, and also..."

Ruthie was pretty sure that the woman's suggestion, while grammatically correct, was anatomically impossible.

MARCH 5

AFTER THE COCKAPOO BITE

SOME PRISSY LADY come in yesterday to tell me I got apostrophes on my sign don't belong there. I ain't usually rude, but I told her where she could put 'em. Sorry, but a cockapoo had just bit me.

But then I kept thinking about it. I ain't really educated, but I like things nice. It was like them apostrophes was mocking me.

So today I got me a razor and started to scrape. I seen her jogging and I thought maybe she'd stop, say *good job*, maybe offer to help. But she turned around and run the other way.

MARCH 6—DENTIST'S DAY

EVERY DAY, MOSTLY

AT 9:20, GABBY's cell *pinged* a reminder. She glanced at the screen: Dentist, 10:00. Instinctively, she ran her tongue around her teeth and thought, *I haven't showered yet.* She couldn't remember the last time she'd flossed.

She scrolled through her contacts for the dentist's number, writing a script in her mind. *I'm not feeling well; mind if I reschedule?* But reluctance to lie moved her to the shower instead. Afterward, she flossed meticulously.

The little bib, the instruments of torture. "Are you flossing every day?" the hygienist asked.

"Oh, sure," said Gabby. "Well, mostly."

The hygienist sighed. "Mmmm-hmmm," she said.

GOING HOME

Since my father died, I've been going home every month or so to help my mother with small projects around the house. Truth be told, they needed doing for years.

"Mark, that last rainfall flooded the woodshed. Could you clean it out?"

I looked down at my white sneakers.

"Wear your father's boots."

I put them on and worked all afternoon, cursing the old man. He had neglected both my mother and this house; she spent their marriage making up excuses.

At home, I seethed, remembering him. Kris tried to calm me; I walked away, still wearing my father's boots.

TOWN COUNCIL

FINALLY—I HAD a writing job. Sure, it was for a local newspaper, issued weekly. But it was *writing*, and I was excited to finally see my name in print.

My first assignment: cover the town council meeting. I took copious notes about trash pick-up schedules, sidewalk repair, the art fair in the park. The article came out a few days later, and with it, a flood of complaints to my editor.

What they printed: *It is now permissible for dog owners to allow their dogs to relieve themselves in public spaces.*

Not. The word was supposed to be *not*.

CAROLE'S HOUSE

CAROLE LIVED IN the same house literally all her life—she was born there, delivered by her frantic father, and she spent fifty-six years of ardent spinsterhood there, surrounded by crocheted doilies and hand-painted greenware.

Then she met Sid, and the walls of Carole's house started to contract.

Tomorrow they will marry. She settles into bed, wondering what it will be like to sleep next to him, picturing his military-spotless bungalow. Carole thought she'd be frightened, but she's not—she was in the womb of this old house far too long. She thinks about tomorrow, when everything will be new.

MARCH 10

SWOON

ALICIA FAINTED AT *anything*. It happened when she saw a bee, when her friend described childbirth, when she tugged at a hangnail.

So when she found herself standing next to an Adonis in the food truck line, she thought, *Gosh, I'd like to swoon into* him. She tried to make it happen, thinking about IV needles. Nothing.

Then the little kid behind her fell. When he held up his bleeding elbow, the swoon came. Alicia aimed at Adonis as she fell.

When she woke, the bleeding kid's mom was dabbing her forehead. Adonis was running, as fast as he could.

MARCH 11

OVERHEARD

FRANNIE WAS IN the bathroom stall when she heard the conversation. It was just a snippet: *Frannie is so ...* Then a toilet flushed, and she missed it. *Frannie is so ... what?* she wondered. *What was she going to say?*

She heard it again in the supermarket. *Oh, that Frannie. She's so ...* A sale announcement drowned out the rest.

It happened five times: at the drive-up bank ... the gas station ... even, crazily, on her radio, interrupted by a burst of static.

I'm so ... what?

She nearly missed the answer, whispered audibly into her spirit. *You're so precious, Frannie. So very, precious.*

MARCH 12

HER FATHER'S SILENCES

WHEN GRACE THINKS about her father, she remembers his silences. How he'd come home and sit in his leather chair, reading the newspaper with an occasional *unh*. How her mother could read his gestures, and would bring him a beer or some ice cream when all he said was, "Patty ..."

Grace remembers the night when she crept downstairs with a stomach ache, stopping halfway when she heard her mother talking with a strange man. They were laughing, saying *darling*, and Grace thought *what if Daddy knew?*

Then she coughed, and her father stepped into the light. "Hey, sweetie," he said.

MRS. CONNOR LEAVES

MRS. CONNOR WOULD probably die today. Ellen stayed away from her bed as much as possible, only coming in occasionally to read the monitor above her head or to ask the gathered family if they needed anything.

When they headed to the cafeteria for lunch, one of them stopped by the ward desk, asked Ellen to check on her.

Ellen stepped into the room, held the old woman's hand. Mrs. Connor's eyes opened—*Oh*, she said. *Oh, look.*

Ellen looked over her shoulder. Nothing to see, just a glimmer of light, a little breeze as Mrs. Connor left the room.

A LITANY OF SUPERLATIVES

THE SHELVES IN Destiny's bedroom are laden with trophies and ribbons, and there is a bookcase filled with scrapbooks. Destiny's mother spends a few hours in the pink room almost every day.

Sometimes Cynthia stands at the trophy wall, touching each gleaming award, remembering each pageant. Sometimes she pulls out a scrapbook and flips through the pages, whispering Destiny's many titles in a litany of superlatives: Little Miss Princess ... Prettiest Tiny Toddler ... Ultimate Grand Photogenic Supreme. The books contain snippets of shimmering fabrics, professional photographs, newspaper clippings.

Only occasionally does Cynthia stop to think: *I wonder where Destiny is now.*

UNDER HER SKIN

THE LIE HAD been festering under Mary's skin for years. On this particular evening, she watched George reading his paper, wiry white hairs sprouting at his wrists, and she was annoyed that he was so oblivious, and so good.

"George." She reached over and tugged the paper so she could see his face. He would be hurt, maybe angry. She would welcome his anger; she deserved it.

"Back in 1972. I lied about ... where I was. You know. That time."

George put down the paper. "Sweetheart, I know."

He stood up and held her shoulders, kissing her until she gasped.

THE LOOK IN HER MOTHER'S EYES

RANDI INTENDED TO get home more often. There was always something more pressing to do, and now it was months since she'd visited.

She and her mother spent a pleasant afternoon playing two-handed bridge. As Randi put the cards away, her mother said, "I wish you'd play the piano. You're so good at it."

"Mom, I haven't played in years. I'd be terrible." But the look in her mother's eyes persuaded her. She sat and played *Amazing Grace*, with far too many mistakes. After the last note, she turned to her mother, shrugging, apologetic.

"Beautiful, dear," her mother said. "Perfect."

HAIR LIKE MINE

I NEVER WENT to no amusement park when I was a kid but when this preacher who knows my P.O. asked some of the guys, I thought *What the hell.*

We were in line for the haunted castle and I was wanting a smoke when I seen this redhead kid. Bout four years old. I couldn't stop looking at him cause of his hair like mine. And cause four years ago between bein' in jail, I signed them papers for the adoption place.

I don't think that kid was mine but I kept watchin' him. Cause he looked real happy.

ACCIDENT PRONE

"SORRY!" SAID HADLEY as she dumped soup in a customer's lap. "I'm so clumsy!"

"Aw, heck," said Hadley as she elbowed the fellow behind her at the deli. "I didn't see you back there."

"Oh, dear," said Hadley, surveying the shattered vase in the department store. "I'll pay for it, of course."

In the elevator on the way home, she shrugged. This had been a rather better day than most.

The doors opened, and a man tumbled in, reaching out for balance and grasping Hadley's bosom in the process. "Well, hey there," she said. A better day than most, indeed.

ON THE SIDEWALK

Now that Barb was alone, she stopped cooking, relying instead on frozen lasagna and deli salads. She stopped reading, too, and spent long hours watching television, deftly clicking the remote without looking at the buttons.

But she didn't stop running; every morning she headed out, covering the same route, not thinking.

Today, however, she slowed to a jog, then stopped, trying to remember why she was running. What was the point?

Perhaps the unexpected chalk squares on the sidewalk had made her stop. She looked down, remembering, almost smiling. She searched for a pebble. Her feet wanted to hop.

THIRTY-ONE YEARS

When the policeman knocked on the door, Edie grabbed her pocketbook. Surely he was collecting for charity; nothing bad ever happened in this quiet neighborhood. She absently fingered her necklace.

"Mrs. Brock, how are you, ma'am?"

"Well, I'm just fine, officer. It's a lovely day, isn't it?"

"It is, ma'am. Mrs. Brock, we've learned something about … about your son."

"About my … about *Johnny*?" She touched the necklace again, a small gold 'J' that she'd worn for thirty-one years. "Henry! This policeman says he knows something about Johnny! Henry!"

Henry didn't turn from his television show. "What's that again? About who?"

COLOR AND LIGHT

When Lydia was seven, she startled the doctor by taking a gasping breath just as he was telling her weeping mother that she had died.

She spent the next eighty years creating exceptional art, a celebrated master of color and light. Lydia never granted interviews; occasionally she told a reporter *it's not right yet.*

And one day she stopped painting, her brush an inch from the canvas. She tilted her head, listening, then set down her brush and walked …

… into another country, where she finally found again the fantastic colors she remembered, from that brief visit so long ago.

BEGINNER'S COASTER

FLO WAS DETERMINED to overcome her fear of roller coasters. "Just let me work my way up to it," she said. "Isn't there a beginner's coaster?"

So she and her daughter sent their husbands away and stood in line at Goofy's Barnstormer. The other mothers there were with toddlers and pre-schoolers. Sasha held Flo's hand. "You'll be fine," she said.

They barely fit in the little cart. When it started moving, Flo buried her head in Sasha's shoulder and screamed.

Fifty-seven seconds later, the cart stopped, and Flo stepped out, ashen and trembling. Behind her, a toddler said, "Again, Mama!"

AN UNFAMILIAR SOUND

WE'D HAD AIDEN since his parents—my brother and his wife—died in an accident. Three months, and Aiden hadn't spoken, but at night sometimes he whimpered for his mother.

On this Saturday, Aiden and I walked to my neighbor's house. Matt was selling his tractor and I thought I'd check it out. We were dickering when Aiden pulled his hand out of mine and pointed toward Matt's porch. I let him go, watched him while we talked.

An unfamiliar sound sent me running toward the porch. There was Aiden, buried in puppies, laughing while his well of sorrow crumbled.

DISCONCERTING

DEBRA TIGHTENED HER shoelaces and looked out the window to see if Sharon was on her porch. Some unfortunate hormonal condition had left Sharon weirdly whiskered and thick of speech. She always wanted Debra to stop and talk, but her eager friendliness was disconcerting.

She was there, on a plastic chair, looking Debra's direction. Debra took the back door.

She think I don't see her peeking at me. She must think I stupid. I don't wanna be best friends or nothing. I just wanna say hey, and nice weather, and was your mail late yesterday cause mine was. That's all.

A LITTLE STRESSED

JANELLE WINCES WHEN Colton asks, "How was your day?"

"Okay," she says. "I'm a little stressed." *I cried for two hours.*

"I hear you," says Colton. "The office is crazy, too. Where's the remote?"

"Isn't three a great age?" Codie and Janelle watch their toddlers at Baby Gym.

"Well …" says Janelle, "I'm exhausted." *Dakota's totally uninterested in potty training, and I can't handle another tantrum.*

"I know, right?" Codie grins. "At least chasing them burns calories."

While Colton snores and Dakota tosses restlessly in his rocket bed, Janelle closes her eyes and whispers, *I'm tired,* hoping that Someone will listen.

PLENTY OF TIME

THE MEETING WAS to begin at 7:00 at a location ten minutes away. It was 6:40 when Paulette gave herself a last look in the mirror. Makeup and hair perfect.

She checked the materials for her presentation. All in order. She glanced at the clock. 6:43. Plenty of time.

Paulette sat and watched a few minutes of *Jeopardy*. She waited for the final question before grabbing her keys and heading for the meeting.

When she entered the room at 7:09, it had already started. Everyone turned to look at her.

"Oh, so sorry!" she said, blushing prettily. "Am I late?"

LAST REHEARSAL

DURING THE LAST rehearsal, Billie messed up her one solo (four notes) and her one line of dialogue. She tore a costume between scenes. Billie played three— no, four—characters in this community production, and during every rehearsal, she found an opportunity to ask her friend (who had six lines of dialogue) *what did you get me into*? Billie was miserable.

When the curtain rose on opening night, she felt, rather than heard, the anticipatory hush of the audience, the quickening of their spirits with the first note of the overture, and her chest filled—not with butterflies, but light.

STILL HERE

MICAYLA JIGGLED THE knob, but it was locked, as she'd expected. The night was warm and still; she could hear her father snoring upstairs through the screen window.

She'd hoped to leave the box inside the door, where they'd find it in the morning, Micayla's way of saying *I'm still here.*

But the door was locked. She set the box on the stoop and looked at the starry sky. It would not rain tonight. Still, Micayla walked to the end of the drive and sat under a tree.

Just in case it got too cold.

In case the baby cried.

A DOZEN SHARPENED PENCILS

VICTORIA LOVED WRITING at her desk, a dozen sharpened pencils and several sheets of slightly stiff paper close at hand. She'd write a few sentences with a satisfying *scritch*; then she'd switch pencils. The sensuousness of those first few words when the pencil was perfectly sharp faded quickly.

Tessie found her mother endearing, but silly. "Mom, you'd get that done much quicker on your computer."

"I know, dear," said Victoria, crossing out a word with a sweeping stroke.

The next day, feeling crabby, Victoria typed an entire letter on the computer. She felt like she was cheating, the whole time.

WINCE

WEARY FROM A relentless day at the clinic, she sank into her office chair and took her notepad. She peeled off the top sheet and wrote in a spiky hand: *Margo Knowles should be excused from work …*

She stopped writing, winced, regarded the note with a twinge of sadness. There was a knock at the door; she jumped, then crumpled the note in one fist.

"Dr. Knowles? About done? We're locking up." The office manager tilted her head. "You okay, Margo?"

"Yes, Hannah. I'm coming."

She tossed the note in the can. The stone in her gut continued to burn.

LAB ASSISTANT

PROFESSOR WINSTON LEFT a note for Caleb, his undergrad assistant: Combine samples 243d and 117g. Lock up when you're done.

Easy enough, thought Caleb. But he hadn't counted on his phone vibrating just as he picked up sample 243d. *Danielle*. He bobbled the sample; it landed upside down. Caleb looked around, scooped up the contents of 243d, and combined them with 117g before checking his text.

That evening, feeling guilty, he went back. Winston wouldn't know—would he?

The new sample was greenish, glowing, and smelled slightly tangy.

Why not? Caleb reached out, with just the tip of one finger—

APRIL

APRIL 1—APRIL FOOL'S DAY

A FAMILY TRADITION

I HAD A HISTORY of picking unsuitable men—but dating Jordan felt *right*. He made me laugh. I was only slightly nervous when he invited me to meet his family over the weekend.

Jordan's brother Jake met me with a bear hug. "Has he told you about the tradition?"

"No … what tradition?"

"It's a family delicacy—here!" He pushed a plate of something unrecognizable at me.

I hesitated, then took a bite. Utterly disgusting.

I struggled to swallow while Jordan and his family cackled. "She actually ate it!" someone said.

Taxi fare home: $55.62. I sent a bill to Jordan.

APRIL 2

FREE, AFTER A FASHION

FIVE YEARS AFTER steel bars had slammed shut behind her, Elise walked out—free, after a fashion. She told them she didn't have a ride; her mother didn't drive. And there was no one else, not anymore. The woman at the front desk called a cab.

"Y'all have a nice day!" she chirped, handing Elise her parcel.

The cab took Elise to her mother's house. The curtains were drawn. She knocked, hesitated, walked in.

They sat in silence, not touching, wanting to touch. Then Elise's mother cleared her throat.

"I made some cookies," she said softly. "Them macaroons you like."

34

OF COURSE I CAN

I HEADED STRAIGHT for New York after fashion school, hoping to design theatre costumes. After a few years off-off Broadway—miles of tulle and sequins, leather and lace—I finally landed a Broadway show.

I thought I was in heaven.

Well, it turns out I was on heaven's front porch. *Real* heaven came to me in the person of Jarrett Gaines, who brought his little daughter backstage to meet me—not one of the actors, but *me*. Jarrett was a widower, Tabitha his world. And now, they are mine.

"Mama," Tabitha said today, "can you make me a Frankenstein tutu?"

TORNADO'S COMING

THE SKY WAS odd—greenish, with a low, dark bank of clouds. She peered outside, then hastily dropped the curtain, rubbing her snarled and aching fingers.

"C'mon, boy," she said, gathering up her little dog, nearly as ancient as she. "I don't like the looks of that weather. Never did like tornadoes."

She gingerly lowered herself into a corner, thankful for her sturdy little house.

When hail started to *ping* against the windows, she covered herself and the trembling dog with a blanket. They stayed there for hours, while she whispered reassurances to her companion. *There's no place like home ...*

AWKWARD

WHEN YOU LIVE in a small village and you're trying to walk five miles a day, sometimes you repeat a circuit. Today my clockwise route intersected with the counterclockwise route of another walker.

1st pass: A mutual nod, meaning: Don't the blossoms smell so nice, and wasn't it a horrible winter?

2nd pass: Well, this is awkward. A glance downward, a wry smile.

3rd pass: How fast is she *going*? A shrug, a grin of shared awkwardness.

4th pass: This is ridiculous. I bend down and pretend to tie a shoelace.

5th pass: I now have a new best friend.

FASHION MAGAZINE

INGRID FLIPS THROUGH the magazine until she finds *her* page. She's posing in a field, and far in the background, some inquisitive cows are looking her way. She wears a dress of some soft lilac material, and she gazes at the camera with hooded eyes.

Standing a few yards behind the camera was a stammering young farmer, the one who had allowed the photographer onto his fields that day.

Ingrid's hands are spotted with age, and callused from decades of working beside that blushing farmer. She looks at the magazine every ten years or so. She made the right choice.

AN EASIER WAY

CLAIRE WATCHED HER mother with amusement. "There's an easier way to make a cake, you know," she said. "Just use a mix."

"This is how I've always done it, dear," said Maxine.

And when Claire saw her mother cutting quilt blocks, she said, "Those come pre-cut, Mom."

"This is how I've always done it, dear," said Maxine.

But when Maxine saw Claire struggling with little Erin's baby carrier—detaching it from the base, hauling it inside, nearly knocking over a plant, an enormous diaper bag slung on her shoulder, she thought, *There's an easier way. Just hold the baby, dear.*

ROADBLOCK

THE CHILDREN MADE it to the bus—barely—with lunches of saltines and over-ripe bananas. Gabe was wearing two different socks.

Melody was sipping her coffee when her phone rang. It was the school secretary; Piper needed picture money today. She grabbed the envelope and ran to the car.

A mile from the school, she saw a police roadblock.

"Ma'am, we're doing random DUI checks. Please step out of the car."

Melody thought about her bralessness, her boxer shorts, her unshaven legs. The chaos at home, the recriminations at school.

"You know what?" she said, "Just take me to jail."

SING ME SOMETHING

JUST BEFORE THEY went into the house, Addy grabbed Sean's arm. "Don't tell my dad you're a rapper. He'd never understand. He's … old. And opinionated."

"What should I tell him, then?"

"Tell him you're a musician. That's not a lie."

Addy's father wasn't buying it. "What kind of musician?" he said, eyeing Sean's sagging pants, his tattoos, his shaved head.

"I'm a singer, sir."

"Sing me something."

Sean hesitated, then stood and cleared his throat. Addy sank into her chair, prepared for humiliation and confrontation.

She wasn't prepared for the beautiful tenor aria, nor for the tears in her father's eyes.

MY SECRET

REAGAN HAD ALWAYS delighted in tattling; I suppose it was her revenge for not being the pretty one. I'd have traded my beauty for her easy charm in a heartbeat.

"Mom!" she'd say. "Mellie took three cookies!" "Mellie got a C on her test!" "Mellie kissed Chad!"

At eighteen, I escaped. Reagan and I exchanged chilly emails for years. When a misdirected email revealed my secret, I dreaded the next Thanksgiving dinner.

"Mom," she said. "Mellie …"

I wadded my napkin in my lap.

"… made a wonderful salad, didn't she?"

I exhaled slowly.

Under the table, Reagan loosened my clenched fingers.

ONE EPISODE EVERY DAY

THERE ARE FIFTY-THREE videotapes on Daisy's shelf, the boxes torn and stained over the years. She keeps them in order; there is one tape for every episode of *Accidental Family*, which ran for two seasons in the '70s.

Daisy watches one episode every day. When Penny, the adorable red-haired star, delivers her precocious dialogue, Daisy leans forward and whispers each line. When Penny is off-screen, Daisy reaches for another bag of potato chips or walks heavily to the kitchen for a carton of ice cream. Sometimes she tucks a hank of hair the color of rusty pipes behind her ear.

REVENGE

I CAME HOME from the hospital with my scars still angry and red. They faded little over the years while I fantasized revenge on the boozy woman whose car kissed mine on a country road. Before the accident, I had only beauty ahead of me: marriage, a happy life. Afterward—nothing. My handsome groom wasn't *quite* strong enough to kiss this ruined face.

Until God.

Until grace.

And there was beauty again—not in my mirror, but in the places of my soul that mirrored beauty.

Today she walked into my church and sat in front of me.

What now?

A RUTHLESS ADVERSARY

I-L-L-L-Y-Y-S. IT WAS a horrible Scrabble rack, until Jill tilted her head and saw the word SILLYLY. A bingo, aaaaand … yes, a spot to play it.

She considered her opponent. The kid looked about eleven, obviously playing out of his league, even in this casual club. His eyes had welled with tears when Jill played WAXEN, sixty-three points.

One table over sat Ed, the club's #1 player, a ruthless adversary. Their eyes met, and Jill blushed. He reached over and patted the kid's shoulder.

"Hey, Uncle Ed," the boy mumbled.

Yesterday, Ed beat her 462-237. She played her bingo.

UNTATTOOED

THAT MORNING, EVERYONE in Mapletown woke with their sins tattooed on their bodies. No amount of scrubbing removed the words: *thief … bigot … liar.*

Many tried to cover them, but there was no disguising words blazoned across foreheads and hands. Eventually, they gave up.

Months later, a stranger came to town, untattooed. He ignored *adulterer* on Michael's cheek and *glutton* on Bethany's palm. He befriended everyone.

Eventually, they came to resent him. How dare he have no visible sins? Incensed, they dragged him outside and stoned him. And as he died, their tattoos disappeared, covering the stranger with *gossip ... drunk ... murderer.*

APRIL 15—TAKE A WILD GUESS DAY

GUESSING GAME

ANOTHER BLIND DATE—we order lunch and then Gary grins at me. "Guess how old I am!"

I despise guessing games. "I don't know ... thirty-four?"

He slaps the table. "Nope! I'm thirty-one. Guess where I grew up!"

The guessing game continues through lunch, and my politeness fades. I guess his first car, his college major, his father's name. When I guess "Hanson" for his favorite band, Gary's grin fades. We finish our salads in silence.

I'm feeling guilty—Gary's not a jerk (like the last guy), and his reddish-blond mustache is charming.

"Hey, Gary?" I say. "Guess my favorite movie."

APRIL 16

PRETTY

THE DRESS WAS pretty, light blue with soft pleats at the waist. It wasn't available in Meredith's size, and it cost more than she had ever spent on one garment.

Nevertheless, after walking past the dress four days in a row, on the fifth day she stepped into the boutique, found the dress in a size 6, and pushed several bills at the cashier.

At home, she stood in front of the mirror, holding the dress close. She twirled once, twice.

Meredith visits the dress a few times each year as it hangs in the closet of her spare bedroom.

APRIL 17—HAIKU POETRY DAY

BIG PAYOFF

EVIE THOUGHT SHE'D lost in the final round of *So You Think You Can Write,* when she had just thirty seconds to come up with a haiku. But in the final seconds, she blurted out:

curiosity
didn't kill me—it was that
horrible schnauzer

Still, it wasn't over until her opponent couldn't correctly conjugate *forego*. Suddenly there were balloons and confetti, and Evie was receiving her million-dollar check.

Actually—she was standing at her mailbox with her first real payment for writing. A fifteen-dollar check from *Denim* magazine. She wondered if it would cover a cappuccino and a chocolate croissant.

APRIL 18

BOOTS

HERB WAS ALMOST out the door when Joanne stopped him. "Dad, wear your boots."

Herb's shoulders slumped. Joanne was too bossy. "I don't need my boots to walk four blocks."

She blocked the door, holding out his boots. "Dad."

He snatched them and fumbled for a bit, then stomped outside, sure that the pretty widows at the library's Senior Night would laugh at him.

Just outside the library, Herb saw Wanda, inexpertly parking by a puddle. He hustled to her door and gallantly held out his arms. "May I?" he said, and lifted her right over the puddle, feeling twenty-three.

APRIL 19

LETTER FROM A SOLDIER

DEAR MOM,

Remember when I was little, and we went to the Independence Day parades? When the soldiers marched by, you told me to stand up and salute. I'd hold the salute until they fired their rifles, then I'd run into the street with a dozen other boys to collect the spent shells. I have dozens of them in a shoebox under my bed.

I don't want them anymore.

I still believe this is a noble cause—but every bullet fired over here is a bullet that's meant to kill someone. Someone who has a mom like you.

Love, Dylan

APRIL 20

TENTH REUNION

I HATE THE way Jeremy is looking at Audra. I've been looking forward to this reunion for months, but I wouldn't have come if I'd known she'd totally monopolize him. I never liked her—always one degree prettier, smarter, more popular than me. All that sickening fake sweetness.

Now Jeremy's dancing with her, and she's got her arm around his waist, like she owns him. This is ridiculous—maybe I should find Derek, dance with him, see if Jeremy even notices …

Jeremy could have had me in a heartbeat, ten years ago. Why'd he have to go and marry Audra?

April 21

RARE CURRENCY

Teagan held her smiles closely, as if they were precious and rare currency. Her laughter she clasped more tightly still; casual acquaintances had never heard her laugh.

So it surprised everyone when she fell in love with Luke. Luke—who intentionally stumbled into parties, landing in the nearest available lap. Luke—whose impossibly accurate impressions were the highlight of every gathering. Goofy Luke, the madcap clown.

At their home, when Luke found himself inexorably drawn into the darkness, he sometimes groped wordlessly for the joy hidden in Teagan's solemn eyes. She held him then, and hummed peace into his soul.

April 22

STALKER

If you look closely at the paparazzi photos of Monica Carlisle (hiding behind huge sunglasses while leaving a party, looking pale and bleary checking in to rehab) you'll find the same man in several of them. He's in the background, often obscured by a visored cap. Fifty-ish, a three-day beard, an old blue windbreaker.

He's been in her pictures for fourteen years, ever since her first explosive role as a nubile teen, and the inevitable scandals that followed.

And if she ever acknowledges him in the crowd, he'll say, "Come on home now, Monica. Your mother and I miss you."

April 23 — Talk Like Shakespeare Day

SHAKESPEARE IN THE PARK

I married up. Everybody says so—it's fine. Suzette's a good sport, and I do hoity-toity stuff with her sometimes. Last night, she tossed this flyer at me, *Shakespeare in the Park*. I guess I grunted.

"It's a comedy," she said. "And you can wear shorts. There's a *concession stand.*"

Sold. We headed out for A Summer Night Dream, or whatever.

I was doing fine, drifting off some, thinking about fishing. But then this actor says, "What sayest thou, bully Bottom?" just when I took a big swig. Sprayed it all over the lady in front of me.

Sorry, Suzette.

APRIL 24—WORLD BOOK NIGHT

AUNT ELAINE'S HOARD

BECAUSE KYLIE WAS Elaine's only living relative, she had the responsibility of clearing her hoard after her death. Kylie was thankful it was a *clean* hoard, unlike some she'd seen on television. Aunt Elaine just had thousands—literally thousands—of books.

Elaine had written one novel in her twenties—a book that the critics loved, but that sold only 2,000 copies. She retreated into her home for six decades.

Kylie was nearly done when she found the letters. They were from another writer, famously reclusive, recently dead. Curious, Kylie started to read.

He had worshipped Aunt Elaine. They never met.

APRIL 25—NATIONAL TELEPHONE DAY

DISTANT VOICES

MIMI'S PHONE RANG at bedtime and she was about to refuse the call, but when she saw that it was her daughter, she picked it up. "Hello?"

No answer, but muffled noises and distant voices.

"Hello? Megan, are you there?"

Now she could hear Megan, talking to someone—was it Ron?—but very indistinctly. The background noise sounded like a restaurant.

"Megan!" Nothing. Mimi could hear laughter, clinking, faint music.

She should have hung up—it was obviously a butt-dial—but she hadn't heard from Megan in weeks. She held the phone to her shoulder and listened for an hour.

APRIL 26

HER LIST OF GRIEVANCES

THE EMAIL WAS the last thing she expected.

She went for months without thinking of him, but when he came back into her thoughts, it was always as a list of grievances. She probed the list as one probes the inside of a bitten cheek—willfully bringing on the pain, perversely pleasurable.

The email was an apology—full of rationalization and justification, but an apology, nevertheless.

She sat down and typed out a reply. *I accept your apology, and I wish you the best.* She hit 'send', then she brought out the list again and added his email to it.

NOW HIRING

My one-gal business had finally picked up enough to hire an assistant. Two applicants—hopefully one would be a good fit.

I brushed crumbs from my blouse and scooped crumpled papers into a drawer as Maisie walked in. She handed me a crisp resume and sat with her ankles crossed, answering every question with ease. *Smooth.* I scraped at a sticky spot on my desk.

Cora stumbled toward me as Maisie left. There was a run in her stockings. Her hair looked mostly unbrushed. She laughed a lot.

Who do you think I hired?

Are you *kidding?* Maisie, of course.

ARBOR DAY

The little village of Twin Elms is proud to have "The World's Largest Arbor Day Parade."

This year, Sheila wants to be the star. She's created a costume of chicken wire and *papier-mâché*—a 12-foot birch. Cleverly placed eye slits are disguised as birch bark, but her view is extremely limited.

She's just passing the judges' stand when she steps on a rock. The tree trunk hobbles her, and she's unable to get her balance. She tilts, stumbles backward, almost rights herself before finally pitching forward, feet wiggling skyward.

"Timber!" says a judge.

As she'd hoped, Sheila was the star.

NOT THAT KIND OF LAMP

At the rummage sale, Gayle picked up a dusty lamp, running a finger along its curves.

"Mother! That's filthy. What are you thinking?"

"It's pretty, Jacquie," she said. "I can clean it."

"*Honestly,* Mother. More junk? Put it *down.*"

"Do you think it might give me three wishes, dear?"

Jacquie sighed heavily. "It's not that kind of lamp. Let's *go.*"

Gayle set the lamp down. Perhaps her hand lingered on the base. Perhaps her lips moved.

The next morning, Gayle opened her door to a furious Jacquie. Three large pimples bloomed on Jacquie's nose. Gayle turned away, hiding a smile.

APRIL 30

THIS TIME

APRIL AND CAMERON went straight home from the fertility clinic, and April lay on the couch, reluctant to walk twenty steps to their bedroom. She was very still, as if her womb were a fragile ornament and any little movement might shatter it.

Cameron sat on the floor, his hand on her belly. After a while, she took his hand and kissed the palm, picturing his beloved oafish fingers cradling their baby's head, tickling a soft tummy, playing this-little-piggy.

It will work this time, she thought. Then she thought it harder, both prayer and command. *This time, it will work.*

MAY

LITTLE BO BEEP

AFTER YEARS OF insomnia, Isabel got a prescription. She slept soundly for several nights, but soon she was troubled by hallucinations: jellyfish in the bathtub, speech bubbles over her husband's head. The doctor told her to discontinue the medication; sleeplessness was better.

A few mornings after she'd taken her last pill, Isabel opened the front door to get the newspaper. A large pink pig was trotting by, followed by a bearded man in a Little Bo Peep outfit.

"Sidney!" she called. "Come quick! Do you see—"

"Well, I'll be," he said. "Doesn't he know Bo Peep had sheep, not pigs?"

SHHH

SHHHH, LITTLE ONE. Shhhh. I have some promises for you on your first day of life, and I need you to listen.

I promise that you may wear your cowboy boots with your princess dress, if you want to.

I promise that you never, ever have to eat beets or liverwurst. Maybe by the time you're grown, the world will be a better place, and no one will ever have to eat them again.

I promise to tell you a new story every day of your life. Until you ask me to stop.

Shhhh, little one. Your mommy's sleeping.

TALENT SHOW

A LITTLE GIRL walked onstage, and Liz, sitting with the other judges, cringed. Another dreadful kid.

The girl started singing—it was the song that had been *their* song, Liz and Eric. Lyrics that spoke of love and longing, desperation and fulfillment. A song no ten-year-old could possibly understand—but the child was nailing it, bringing Eric acutely back, making Liz's throat actually ache.

She looked at the other judges' sheets—all 10s. Liz hated the thought of this child, this song, winning the talent show—but every note was perfect. She took her pen, sighed, and entered a score.

MAY 4

ONE ESSAY

ALICE SITS AT her desk, where a mug of coffee creates a ring on the old oak. There is a messy stack of papers nearby—the 7th grade contest essays she was asked to judge.

She reads them with impatience, even dismay. What are they *teaching* them these days? She tosses aside any essay that contains *alot* or *cuz*. She makes disapproving noises; the cat jumps up to investigate, sending a dozen essays to the floor.

Alice doesn't care. She's clutching one essay full of scratchings and erasures, and her heart is thumping wildly. A tear glistens on her cheek.

MAY 5

NO MOURNING TODAY

"DOESN'T THAT BIRD sound like it has lips, Shawna? HOOoo-oo-oo."

"What bird is it, Mama?"

"A morning dove."

In seventh grade, Shawna wrote a poem about the dove.

Her mother's imagery always made her laugh; the morning dove was her favorite sound.

Her teacher returned it with this note:

The correct spelling is 'mourning' dove.

How appropriate, Shawna thought, that she should hear a mourning dove today. She hadn't heard one in years. But she would not mourn today; her mother would not wish it.

She put on her black dress and veil, and laughed about the bird with lips.

HI, KIDS!

IT TOOK AN hour for Sylvia to put on all her makeup. She had to be very precise: a heart under her left eye, highly arched brows, exaggerated geisha lips. Then there was the hair—thirteen braids, tied in multicolored ribbons. Lederhosen. Peasant blouse. Striped socks. Combat boots. Sylvia woke at six in order to be ready in plenty of time.

When she finally had her boots laced, she stood at the full-length mirror, practicing her miming. Then she sat on her porch waving to schoolchildren, who whimpered and clutched their mothers' hands.

Maybe today, someone will need a clown.

TALKING TO CISSY

PASTOR LEVINE GOES to his tiny church early—6:00 most days, when the sky is barely lightening.

Every morning, he sees Claude Dorset in the little church cemetery, sitting against a tombstone that says CICELY DORSET, BELOVED WIFE. The first time he saw Claude there, he went to him, offered him coffee.

"No, pastor," said Claude. "I'm just talking to my Cissy. I'll be moving along."

So Pastor Levine leaves him be. Except today, he feels pulled to the cemetery, to see again if he can help.

Claude's not here, though—he's with his Cissy, leaving only his body below.

STUPID, STUPID

ELIOT SEEMED UTTERLY uninterested in Julianne, despite her efforts to engage him in conversation. She'd stop by to ask for a folder or to use his stapler; he'd hand the item to her silently, then turn back to his computer.

Too bad, she thought. *I just wanted to be friends.*

On this Tuesday, she entered the storage room to look for some headphones. She was about to leave when she heard his voice, back in the corner:

"Would you do me the great honor ... *dang,* Eliot. *Stupid, stupid.* Hey, Julianne, let's grab some grub ... *Stupid.*"

She slipped quietly out, blushing.

MAY 9

MURDER PARTY

HARPER LOVED DEVON, but she found his friends dull, dull. Their idea of a good time was *hours* of wine and politics.

"Devon, let's throw a murder mystery party!" she said. He knew it wouldn't fly, but he loved her, too.

Invitations were sent, with special instructions to the murderer and the victim.

The guests trickled in, only a few wearing the suggested costumes.

The victim was an hour late. "So sorry," she said. "Nanny crisis."

"Do I kill her now or wait a bit?" said the murderer.

"Oh, never mind," said Harper, with actual murderous thoughts. "Who brought wine?"

MAY 10

HALF A BEAT TOO LATE

MARLA'S OFFICE DIDN'T have a dress code, but the women dressed in somber suits. Marla wore flowered dresses and blouses with splashes of bright color.

At lunch, her co-workers picked at leafy salads, while Marla enjoyed cheeseburgers, or sometimes a slice of cake with ridiculous frosting.

In conversation, Marla was always half a beat too late, several decibels too loud.

At home, she'd find Terry and sit on the floor, hugging his knees. "Tell me again why you love me," she'd say.

"Because there's no one like you, my onliest," said Terry, and he coaxed her up into his arms.

MAY 11

A LONER BY NATURE

I DON'T EVEN know his name. This is a small town, and I see him all the time, out and about. Our morning walks often intersect, and we always exchange brief, friendly glances.

Sometimes I've seen him in the park, hanging out with his friends, while I try to concentrate on my book.

He's slender, fair, with dark expressive eyes. Always impeccably groomed; I like that in a fellow.

Sometimes I imagine living with him.

I'm a loner by nature, but it might be nice to wake up to a friendly face like his. I think I'd name him "Rascal."

GERTRUDE'S PHOTOGRAPH

GERTRUDE HOBBLED THE length of her driveway. A dog sniffed around her mailbox, and she poked it with her cane, sending it yelping toward home.

She riffled through the mail, scowling. A kid bicycled by; she scowled at him, too.

That afternoon, the Dial-A-Ride van arrived five minutes late, and Gertrude muttered darkly at the driver. When he returned her home, he hopped out and offered his arm. She shoved him away with her handbag.

At bedtime, Gertrude picked up a photograph of a handsome young man in uniform. She held it to her breast, humming an old, old song.

COMMUTER TRAIN

SHE WAS READING, waiting through the fourteen stops this train would make before her stop downtown. So far—uncharacteristically—no one had taken the seat next to hers.

A shadow darkened the pages of her novel, and she sighed and scooched toward the window, not looking up. But the shadow passed, and a card dropped in her lap. It was engraved with her name, an address in the city, and a time later that afternoon.

She turned around, but nobody was there—just the usual bored and snoozing commuters. She looked at the card again.

She's probably going to go.

SHE WAS THE ONE

ADRIAN AND VALERIE had only been dating for a month—just two dates—when she invited him to her 40th birthday party. He didn't hesitate; he didn't know Valerie very well, but he had a feeling she was *the one*.

Valerie was nervous. She'd never had a boyfriend, wasn't sure how she'd act with Adrian and her family in the same room.

Adrian was late, but he finally showed up with an enormous wrapped box and a goofy grin.

"Wow!" Valerie said. "That's huge! Hope it's not one of those box-in-a-box-in-a-box thingies!"

She giggled self-consciously.

But it was. Poor Adrian.

MAY 15

SECOND CHANCES

WHEN I BROKE the Unforgivable Commandment, my parents kicked me out. I found peace in a city hundreds of miles away, and figured out how to live a compassionate life. I fell crazy in love with Rory, and then I fell crazy in love with the God of second chances.

And then I learned that Grandpa was dying. I flew home, an ache in my chest.

At the hospital, my parents sidled out of Grandpa's room. I took his hand, and he pulled me near. I bent closer, ignoring his indescribable breath.

"Casey," he whispered, "I always loved you best."

MAY 16

SOCIAL SITUATIONS HOMEWORK

MISS TAYLOR GAVE me Social Situations homework. Ride the subway, observe faces, and figure out the emotions.

The lady across from me is pink and her baby is brown. She might be a kidnapper, but she doesn't look like a criminal. No gun.

"Hey," I say. "That baby looks just like you."

Her eyes get round, then she smiles and says *Thank you*. I see a tear on her face.

I don't know what emotion is round eyes, a smile, and a tear, but I didn't tell a lie. They both have eyes, nose, mouth, feet. Their hands look soft.

MAY 17

IN THE ATTIC

MAURA HAD NEVER been up above the garage before; Clyde always took care of lugging things up there. The big suitcase. The turkey roaster. But Clyde was gone now, and she needed the picnic basket.

She could do this.

She leaned the ladder against the breezeway wall, then tentatively started to climb. She pushed the hatch with an *oof*, then somewhat ridiculously clambered with knees and elbows into the tight space. Her elastic waistband snagged on the hatch, and her granny panties flashed, but no one saw.

Outside, a big truck seismically rolled by, jostling the ladder from the wall.

CITY GIRL

ERICA LEFT THE city for the first time in years to attend a reunion in Nebraska for a distant branch of the family. It would be fun, she thought.

She hadn't anticipated the sturdy cheerful women in stretch pants and flowered blouses, the loud men in baseball caps. She was baffled by Jell-o molds and mayonnaise-y salads. She squawked when a daddy longlegs sauntered toward the deviled eggs.

Most of all, Erica was unprepared for the dizzying open sky, the unbroken flat horizon. She longed for skyscrapers, honking taxis, the buzz of overheard conversations. *How do people live like this?*

11TH GRADE ENGLISH, JOURNAL—WHO DO YOU ADMIRE?

I ADMIRE MY mother for being classy enough to drink out of the glass instead of the bottle. And she almost always waits until afternoon to start.

I admire my dad for his list of "50 ways to avoid involvement in your kid's life." He could go pro at staying away.

I admire my brother for his record time for getting kicked out of college. He lasted nine days.

I admire *me* for writing this journal, when I'd rather be grabbing my sister out of class because of the cigarettes I found in her backpack.

Do you even read these?

SWATHED IN TAFFETA

MY MOTHER'S FAVORITE wedding picture is a neck-to-knees close-up of her, swathed in taffeta. She's holding a bouquet of white roses and stephanotis, and wearing gloves with pearl buttons at the wrist.

Tellingly, my father is not in the picture, just as he was absent for most of their thirty-seven years.

"Mom, why did you save this?" I toss the picture in her lap. "Doesn't it remind you of your awful marriage?"

"Awful?" She holds the picture up, then traces the outline of her flowers. "No, it was never *awful*. When your father was here, he made me feel … beautiful."

MAY 21

JOB INTERVIEW

HOW WAS THE interview?

It was terrible! I actually used the word 'irregardless'.

That's not so bad.

For a marketing job? It's horrible. And then I got the hiccups.

I'm sure no one noticed.

Oh, they noticed. They got me water. One of them even said 'boo'.

Well … if you don't get the job, that would be okay, wouldn't it? We wouldn't have to move. You love this place.

No, you love this place. This was my dream job. I've wanted it for years.

Should he tell her they called, right before she came home?

He *really* loves this place.

MAY 22

LAST CHANCE

IAN'S SOCKS WERE on the floor, near the hamper but not in it. It would have taken him exactly no effort to actually hit the hamper. Rita stormed into the den.

"This is your last chance, buddy. I swear, if I see socks on the floor one more time—"

Ian gazed at her thoughtfully, then walked to the door. "Don't worry, Rita. It won't happen again."

"I can't believe he left me!" Rita wailed to her best friend. "He was such a sweet guy."

"Yeah," said Lorena. "And after all the guys you've had. He mighta' been your last chance."

MAY 23

GRANT SHOULD HAVE KNOWN

Hey

Hey yourself

I'm glad Grant introduced us

Me too
So … wanna go out sometime?
Sure.
Free for lunch tomorrow?
Yeah.
Noon at MacRee's?
Could we go someplace else?
You don't like MacRee's?
It's too busy. Public.
Maybe the Sammich House?
Still too public.
You don't want to be seen with
me?
Well …
Are you MARRIED?
No!
What is it then?
Do you always wear that hat?
Yeah. I'm a huge Harriers fan.
I'm not.
Really not.
My family would KILL me if
they saw me with a Harriers
fan.
Know what? I've got plans for
lunch.
Whatever. Me too.

MAY 24—INTERNATIONAL TIARA DAY

PRINCESS

ARIANNA YAWNED, ROLLED over, drowsily called out.

"Yes, my princess?" Gregory appeared at the doorway.

"I'm awake," she said.

He disappeared, but moments later, he brought her breakfast: sliced fresh peaches, lightly dusted with sugar.

"Mmmm," she murmured, yawning again. "Just a few minutes more, Gregory." She curled back up, waving him away.

When she woke again, Gregory was gone, but he'd left a yellow flower next to her bed.

She hurried to pull on her dress, smiling at Gregory's thoughtfulness. Just before heading out, she tucked the flower into her bosom—right next to her nametag from Dinah's Diner.

MAY 25—INTERNATIONAL MISSING CHILDREN'S DAY

MISSING, NEVER FOUND

LETTERS TO THE editor in this village aren't typically earth-shattering. Complaints about baggy-pantsed skateboarders. Dogs barking. Too many snow days, or not enough of them—that sort of thing.

So I was surprised to see this one on my computer: *I think I went to first grade in your town. I remember my teacher, Mrs. Cherry. That was thirteen years ago. I think I remember a big clock near the library. My name was Jennica then.*

I've only been here five years, but my secretary remembered. Jennica Randall and her father—missing, never found. Her mother still lives here, waiting.

MAY 26

THREADBARE

SUE TOOK HER friend's hand. "Come out with us tonight," she said. "You can't spend your whole life in this house."

"Maybe tonight he'll come home." Dianne pulled her hand away. "Thanks, but I'll stay here. Go on without me."

After Sue left, Dianne made a cup of tea. She took it to her chair by the window, the one with threadbare arms. She pushed the curtain aside and whispered his name.

He didn't come home that night, but he came closer than he'd come in months. He saw the curtain, the shadows of movement as she stirred her tea.

MAY 27

BATHROOM MIRROR

JEANNE SHUFFLED TO the bathroom and peered, bleary-eyed, into the mirror. There were spatters of toothpaste speckling the glass, and Jeanne gave a huff of exasperation. She'd asked Bernie to clean up his mess—honestly, she couldn't fathom how he managed to hit the mirror with his spit. Did he aim right *at* the mirror?

She stepped into the shower, mumbling. *Fifty-two years …*

When she pushed the curtain aside seven minutes later, there was Bernie, using his finger to draw a heart in the steam coating the mirror. He turned to grin at her; she shed her exasperation like droplets.

VISUAL AID

HOLLY GRIPPED THE vase, wanting badly to throw it at Cal's head. Instead, she dropped it on the floor, where it shattered into dozens of lethal-looking shards. She stepped past the shards, the spreading water, the wilting flowers, and stood at the door, thinking of an exit line.

"Some things can't be repaired once they're broken, Cal." She nodded at the floor, weirdly happy that she'd created a visual aid. "You made this mess—you clean it up." *Good one,* she thought.

When she returned later, still angry but needing her cell phone, Cal was patiently gluing the ruined vase.

ROSE'S WELCOME SPEECH

FINALLY—NEW NEIGHBORS next door. Rose pulled the cookies from the oven, already rehearsing her welcome speech. She'd definitely tell them about the Davidson's dog … and of course, she'd invite them to church right away. The very thought made Rose's fingers tingle. She grabbed last week's bulletin out of her Bible.

She piled a plate with still-warm cookies and rang the neighbors' doorbell with an expectant smile.

When the door opened, the smile faded from Rose's face and she fumbled with the cookies. "Oh! *Here,*" she said, thrusting the plate forward. She fled with the bulletin still in her hand.

DIARY

AMY BOUGHT THE old books at a rummage sale—fifty cents each. She lugged the box home and sat on the floor to sort through the titles. She was surprised to find a diary there, with a silly and ineffective lock. She set the diary aside for later.

Should I? She thought. The diary's writer was probably long gone.

It felt *wrong*, but eventually curiosity won out.

She popped the lock off with a table knife.

**You broke the lock.
What gives you the right to read my private thoughts?
Close this book … immediately.**

Awesome. Amy settled in to read.

May 31—Save Your Hearing Day

BOOMING BASS

Julie pulled up to the red light, annoyed at the booming bass coming from the car in the next lane. She could feel her throat vibrate with each note. Gripping the wheel, she willed the light to change.

Don't they know that'll destroy their hearing? I bet it's one of my students.

Unable to shake that last thought, Julia glanced over. *I'll give him a piece of my mind on Monday.*

He was drumming his steering wheel and singing—with gusto, it seemed. He was so hunched over that his sparse white hair barely skimmed the top of the wheel.

JUNE

ONE SHOE

THEY NEEDED THIS trip—Josh had been annoying recently. Shana longed for depth; Josh was always so darned flippant.

"Shana, I've been thinking."

At last. "Yes?"

"You ever wonder why you sometimes see one shoe on the road?"

Shana sighed. "No."

"Well, I figured it out. Gimme a shoe."

"What?"

"Just do it."

She pulled off her sandal and held it out. Josh said, "This is why." He tossed it out the window, grinning. "Gotcha!" He was still laughing as he turned the car around.

Shana shrank into her seat, hoping she could still cancel the florist and the photographer.

JUNE 2

PARABOLA

THEIR FATHER DIED in November, and it was months before the Simpson siblings could spread his ashes as he'd asked.

They met at his favorite place on a warm June day—the park where he'd played chess, a frequent and cheerful loser.

There was a pleasant silence, then Tim took the urn from Jillian, flinging the contents upward. There was no breeze. The ashes traced a perfect parabola, then landed in an intact little pile at their feet. They looked at each other, stifling laughter.

When they left the park, the tips of their shoes were still a bit ashy.

VALEDICTORIAN

ASHLEY STOOD TO deliver her valedictory address. She was not nervous. She'd submitted a speech to the principal a few days earlier, and he'd approved it, patting her shoulder as he handed it back to her. "We're proud of you, Ashley," he said.

That speech was now crumpled in the trash can outside Mr. Hartman's office. She'd memorized her *real* speech.

"Parents, teachers, administration—welcome. I'm here tonight to say that despite what you've heard—cheaters sometimes prosper." She took her seat, looking straight ahead.

The audience, programmed to applaud, clapped their hands once or twice, incredulity shadowing their faces.

JUNE 4

SPIRITUALIST

I LIKE TO call on plain women; they love the attention. But this one—she seems to know all my tricks.

"I feel someone significant … maybe the name starts with J, or M?" There's always a J or an M.

"I can't think of anyone," she says. Her eyes say *Go ahead, keep trying.*

"I'm hearing … maybe a grandmother? Someone who's passed?" There's always a dead relative.

She shrugs. "Nope."

Another few rounds, and I feel the audience turning. *Can this guy do a reading or not?*

Why'd she have to come, this homely woman clutching her clunky cross necklace?

JUNE 5

ENOUGH

YOU'RE AN APPRENTICE genie?

Yeah—so no loopholes. No more wishes, no more genies. Just one smallish wish.

Will I regret this later?

Probably.

How much time do I have?

A minute.

Okay, I wish for ... enough. Enough food, money, clothes—and *love*. Enough happiness. Enough peace. Enough ... everything.

That shouldn't be difficult. That's all? Just—enough?

Well, for my whole family.

I can do that.

Promise?

Promise.

Then you'd better get a senior genie to help.

Why?

My whole family. Think about it ...

Whoa. That's ... everybody in the world, isn't it?

Yup. Thanks! I think ... that might be enough.

UP

THE OLD MAN hadn't spoken in days, but there it was. *Up,* he said. His startled nurse elevated his bed and plumped his pillows, but he raised a feeble hand and shook his head. *Up.*

She found an orderly, and together they wheeled the old man to the fifth floor solarium. He gazed out for a moment, then said it again. *Up.*

The nurse shrugged and took the old man to the roof, where employees sometimes smoked. He turned his face to the sun, grinning. Then, with exceeding gracefulness, he raised his palms to the sky and flew away home.

CONNIE'S GARDEN

JASON EXPECTED THAT Connie would plant a garden that first spring. Women in his family always gardened.

With trepidation, Connie purchased seeds, gloves, tools. She clawed at a patch of dirt and timidly dropped in a few seeds, then drowned them from the quaint red watering can she'd adored at the store.

Miraculously, a few plants grew.

Connie occasionally pulled what she hoped were weeds, yipping a little when she saw a worm or when dirt stained her pretty gloves.

Her garden yielded two meager salads. Jason looked at the plates, kissed her soundly, and took her out to dinner.

BLIND DATE

TERI AND JOE fidgeted at their booth, the expectations of a blind date looming large.

"So …" said Teri. "What exactly does an agricultural microbiologist do?"

"Well, I study microorganisms that affect crops. It sounds boring …"

Teri made a small noise that could have meant anything.

"… but it's actually cool. Last week, I discovered a new species of nematode that …"

"Nema*what?*"

The date was over before it began. Teri left after one coffee. Joe lingered, dispirited. He didn't notice the girl from the next booth leaving, until she dropped a note on his table:

Nematodes are hot Call me! Sarah 555-3144

LASER

"SO YOU WANT a tattoo removed?" I said. The guy across from me was as sad a guy as I'd ever seen. He pushed up his sleeve. The tat was a heart, with *Tanith* in elaborate script.

Tanith.

"She's my wife. She cheated on me, man. It's over."

Tanith—it's an unusual name. How many could there be, in a town this size?

I remembered her. She'd been sorry before the next morning. She cried, said she loved her husband; this was a big mistake. When she put her head on her arms, the tears ran down her freckled shoulders.

IT'S SOME DAY

BEVERLY LAY IN bed, thinking about pea-sized blobs of toothpaste, darned socks, and thermostats set at 65. She poked Paul in the ribs. "It's some day," she said.

Paul opened an eye. "It's Saturday. Go back to sleep."

"No, I said *some* day. We've been scrimping all our lives for *some day*. Well, it's here."

Paul was really awake now. "Are you all right? Is it …"

"I'm fine. But we're not getting any younger. Let's do it while we still can."

They flew to Greece, drank wine, danced with the locals. They used a full inch of toothpaste, every time.

A TINY SCAR

IT WAS SUCH a tiny scar, really. A minor accident, a cut requiring three stitches. The plastic surgeon was excellent, and Stephanie's lip now had only a thin pale line hugging that little groove.

She'd developed a habit, though, of covering her mouth with her hand.

Jeff found it charming. She seemed coy, flirtatious, only kissing him in semi-darkness. But then it was less charming—an unnecessary affectation. "It's not even noticeable," he'd say.

Stephanie tried to keep her hand from her mouth, but it fluttered there, unbidden. He would catch her hand, kiss it, hold it to his chest.

FREE PASSES

FROM MY TICKET window at Millie's Mini-Golf, I can watch the first hole (the loop-de-loop) and the last. I like to observe the single dads. Most of them hurry their kids through each hole, encouraging them to flout the rules: they use their putters like hockey sticks, or simply drop the ball into the cup.

But some dads stand behind their kids, patiently molding their small hands around the putters. They take practice swings, and say, "Nice try, buddy."

When the nice dads return their pencils, I give them free passes. Maybe someday, one of them will become a regular.

UNDER TABLES IN THE BASEMENT

WHEN DONNY AND I were kids, our dad was an itinerant preacher. Sometimes we went with him, and after the service and the potluck, when Dad was talking to the people, Donny and I would explore the church.

After a while, Dad would call out, "Donny! Lizzy! Let's go!" and we'd crawl out from under the tables in the basement.

When Donny tells it, Dad was searching frantically for us, and we were hopelessly lost in dark places inhabited by bats and spiders. When he found us, our Dad wept for joy.

I wish Donny's version was the true one.

JUNE 14

WEARY

THERE WOULD BE more room for groceries if Taffy and Zach would walk, but Lila was tired of pulling them away from the tempting lower shelves. She plopped them into the basket, piling Pull-Ups and juice around them, with a weary admonition about opening the crackers.

When Zach opened the box with his dimpled fingers and swiveled away from his sister, she swatted his shoulder. "Mom!" said Taffy, her little hand in a fist.

Lila grabbed the crackers and tossed them away, then smacked Taffy's head, hard. "What have I told you?" she said. "We don't *hit* in this family."

JUNE 15

CONSIDERABLY OLDER NOW

CARRIE HAD BEEN looking for love since she was twelve, and she'd papered her bedroom with posters of barely-pubescent celebrities. She was considerably older now, and love had eluded her.

She tried the Make Carrie Beautiful plan, but lacked the prerequisites, being somewhat plump and blotchy. So she worked on Make Carrie Interesting, taking a role in a community production of *Oklahoma!* There she met Keith, a cowboy in the chorus. At last—love.

They stood backstage, holding hands while Laurey and Curly sang.

"I love you," said Carrie.

"Me, too," replied Keith. "Ninth grade is going to be *awesome.*"

JUNE 16—WORLD SEA TURTLE DAY

BLISS

JANE GOES TO the beach after the gaudy display of sunset has faded. She prefers the deepening sky, the long shadows of scrubby vegetation, the breath of waves on the shore. A blanket is in her bag, and a few ripe plums.

She looks out on the water for a long time, mostly not thinking at all. There is a sort of bliss to her oblivion.

After a while, she gathers the blanket around her shoulders and rests her head on the sand. She's awakened later by a susurration near her face: thousands of tiny sea turtles, flailing toward home.

EARLY MORNING CAULIFLOWER

I DON'T MIND working the late shift, letting the ones with families work days. It's quiet here at 2 a.m., and I can think. Not that my thoughts are profound or anything. I mostly write music in my head. I just like it quiet.

There's this guy who comes in sometimes. He wanders around, and then he picks up something random. Like a cauliflower. What needs cauliflower at 2 a.m.?

But he seems nice. He has a kind smile. He doesn't say anything. Just slides me whatever he's buying, and that nice smile. Today I think he almost said *hello*.

PICNIC WITH MARCO

CORAL PACKED THE picnic hamper with Marco's favorites: a crusty baguette, soft goat cheese, a cluster of tiny grapes, tender coconut macaroons. She set out for their meeting place in the meadow with a quickening heartbeat. Their last meeting had been weeks ago.

After spreading the white cloth, she sat, smoothing her skirt, waiting. When he came to her, it was with a whisper as quiet as the breeze. *My dearest.* He reached out, gently sweeping her hair behind one ear.

"Hey, Mom," said Robbie, grabbing a soda from the cooler. "There's some crazy lady over there, talking to herself."

THE PIRATE

TATE HOLDS TIGHTLY to Mommy's hand. Once, at the supermarket, he had let go when he saw cereal with Legos inside. He'd grabbed the box, wanting to ask could she *please* buy it, and Mommy was gone.

So now he holds on, even when they're standing in line at the bank. But the line isn't moving, and Tate is bored. He looks around, then tugs Mommy's sleeve.

"Look, Mommy, there's a pirate!"

She turns, sees the fellow with the eye patch. "I'm so sorry," she says, but the man smiles, crouches to Tate's level.

"Shiver me timbers!" he says. "Arrrrrrr!"

IT WAS JIGGLYPUFF

MARIE SAW THE quiz on her friend's Facebook wall: What Is Your Ideal Career? *This looks fun,* she thought, and she answered ten silly questions. When 'pet psychic' popped up on the screen, she clapped in delight and looked for more quizzes.

That afternoon, she discovered her Klingon name (M'Kota), her romantic style (Casablanca), the color of her aura (teal), and her survival time in the Zombie apocalypse (1:34 minutes).

She was working on "What Pokemon Are You?" when someone knocked at the door.

"We haven't seen you all day," said Cara. "They're serving dinner. Do you need your walker?"

MOTORCYCLES

THERE WAS STILL one basket left to hang on the clothesline, and Michelle's arms ached. She was reaching for a pair of jeans when the ground started to rumble. *Earthquake,* she thought, and she knelt and placed her palms on the ground as if to stop it.

It was not an earthquake. Dozens—perhaps hundreds—of motorcycles came roaring past her yard, many with two riders, women with their arms loosely wrapped around the drivers' waists. Some of the motorcyclists waved.

Michelle didn't really want to go with them—but she wanted to be the type of girl who *would.*

TATTOO

YOU'LL REGRET GETTING a tattoo, her mother had said. How's it going to look when you're old and wrinkly? And you're only eighteen—there'll be lots of boys. How will *they* feel when they see his name?

But she'd done it anyway. A heart wrapped in a Celtic knot, with a banner reading "Daniel." On the curve of her left breast, just above her heart.

Now she lay on her side next to Daniel, her breath ruffling his meager white hair. Through her thin nightgown, she could see the tattoo, faded and wrinkled. She didn't regret it, not one bit.

JUNE 23 — PINK FLAMINGO DAY

FLAMINGOS

SOMEONE HAD PLANTED a plastic flamingo in Gillian's yard, looking right into her window. She yanked it up with a scowl.

Next morning, there were a dozen, peeking into her car. She uprooted them and laid them on the grass.

On day three, she peeked outside, wondering. Beak-to-beak flamingos filled her lawn. A narrow, flamingo-less path led to her car.

When she got home, they were gone. They didn't appear for days, and Gillian felt mildly disappointed.

But one morning there was a trail of them leading down the street. She laughed out loud and ran to get her shoes.

JUNE 24

STRAWBERRIES

FRANK ENJOYS HIS little strawberry field. It yields enough berries for a booth in the Farmer's Market, and for three weeks in June, he posts a "You Pick" sign at the road. Shirley watches the pickers with narrowed eyes, and swoops in whenever someone eats more than one or two off the vines.

But Frank doesn't mind. He always searches for a solemn little kid, someone who looks to his mother for permission before eating a berry. When he finds that kid, he takes an extra quart to their car after they've paid. "Here," he says. "Sweets for the sweet."

JUNE 25

HER MOTHER'S VOICE

THE TEACUP WAS hidden toward the back of a glass case, behind a knobby butter dish. Josie almost missed it, but something made her stop and turn around. It was beautiful: pink roses, a gold rim.

"I'd like to see that cup," Josie said, and when the woman handed it to her, she held it to her chest. Her fingers trembled — too many memories. This could have been her mother's cup.

When she got home, Josie opened the tissue paper. Her mother's voice whispered in her ear. She placed the cup on the floor and ground it carefully to pieces.

JUNE 26

THE OFFICER SMILES

[SHERRY SITS ON her bed, fully clothed. One wrist is handcuffed to the bedpost. There is a knock at the door.]

You called 911, ma'am?

Yes! Please help—

[She indicates her manacled hand. The officer smiles.]

It's not what you think! I don't even have—they're for my *nephew*. He's learning *magic*. I just wanted to see if they work.

Where's the key?

On my dresser with all the packaging. Thank you so much. I'm so embarrassed …

No problem, ma'am. [He finds the key] *But first, let me just …*

[He takes the cuff and slides it up over the bedpost.]

JUNE 27

NOT YET

SAMMIE CHECKS THE address on her work order from Maid Easy. She's nervous, but determined to do a good job, to make it work this time. She feels fancy in her uniform with its crisp collar and white buttons. It's too bad, she thinks, that it has to share a drawer with her old wardrobe, not yet replaced—the tiny skirts and tight halter tops, the ripped stockings.

At the house, she's scrubbing a marble countertop when the owner walks in, a man who Sammie immediately recognizes. She bows her head and keeps scrubbing, wondering if she'll ever be clean.

JUNE 28

NOT THAT MAN ANYMORE

TROY IS VAGUELY aware that someone's working in his kitchen, but a lifetime habit of rendering servants invisible is seated in his soul. He stands just inside the door, fiddling with his phone, when the maid gasps.

She looks familiar, and his mind scrolls through a few crazy and unlikely scenarios—*one of Morgan's friends? Someone from the meetings?*

And then he *knows* who she is, and he wants to go to her, to apologize, to tell her he's not that man anymore. She is vigorously bleaching the countertop, and Troy wishes that she could somehow make him clean, too.

BEETLE

EARLY MORNING. RACHEL sees the bug—black, probably a beetle—near the bathroom. It's waving its antennae at her. She stays on the couch, eyeing it, through hours of morning television.

12:13 p.m. It hasn't crawled away, but it's still mocking her. The dog sniffs it, uninterested. Perhaps it's mostly dead; usually Rufus plays with insects until they're fatally exasperated.

3:41 p.m. Still there. Rachel takes her heaviest coffee mug and steels herself to trap it; Hank will kill it later. She tiptoes toward the beetle, brandishing the mug.

It's a button from her raincoat, with a few loose threads.

PHOTO ALBUM

LUCY WAS AT a rummage sale when she spotted the photo album. The pictures had been removed; she could see their outlines, three on each page.

She paid a quarter for the album and took it home. There she discovered two pages stuck together; when she teased them apart, there were three pictures. A balding middle-aged man holding up a large fish. In front of a red 1968 Mustang. With his arm around a cute little girl.

Lucy likes to imagine she's the woman who took the pictures. She has created elaborate memories with the fellow, who she's named Vince.

JULY

JULY 1 — POSTAL WORKER DAY

PLACES HE'S NEVER BEEN

DWAYNE LOVES BEING a mailman. Twenty-nine years of walking the village in a day have given him fine, muscular calves, but his shoulders are lopsided from the mailbag.

He misses *real* mail: creamy envelopes with slanted, ink-splotched handwriting, penciled letters addressed to *Grandma Willis*.

Most of all, he misses postcards—their glossy pictures of places he's never been, their jaunty greetings.

When Dwayne gets home, he tosses his bag aside and reaches for an old shoebox. He closes his eyes and shuffles through hundreds of cards, pulling out a picture of a seaside sunset. *Hi, June! We're having a blast!*

JULY 2 — WORLD UFO DAY

SCIENCE

SHE COVERED THE screen of his device and made him look at her. "Don't you believe in anything?" she said. "Nothing mysterious or … unexplained?"

"I believe in *us*. I believe in science. That's all I need."

She was a scientist, too—but sometimes she felt a longing for magic. And she wanted an explanation for what she'd seen in the sky last night. Something bright and blinking—something obviously not natural—passing through the shadow of the third moon.

She'd gone to her highest powered instruments and observed it for hours, trying to decipher the meaning of the markings: NASA.

JULY 3 — COMPLIMENT YOUR MIRROR DAY

MIRROR

THE MIRROR LEANED against the back wall of the shop, covered with an old towel. Jennifer threaded her way through a furniture maze to examine it closer.

68

Mr. Abernathy grabbed her arm. "That's a very special piece." He looked around, then whispered, "It shows you as you really are."

Jennifer snorted, but she bought the mirror.

Once home, she hung it in a back hall, laughing at her reluctance to actually look in it.

As you really are ...

Two days later, she stood at the mirror, expecting warts, green skin. But she saw herself as utterly beautiful, bathed in light.

JULY 4—INDEPENDENCE DAY (UNITED STATES)

REVOLUTIONARY

THEODORE HAD BARELY begun his lecture on "Seeds of Revolution in the American Colonies" when he was distracted by a woman in the fourth row. Pretty. Fifty-ish. Listening intently, taking notes. Often she smiled, even appeared to chuckle. Theodore was nonplussed by her; his lecture was not particularly amusing.

Afterward, he rushed to seek her out. She took his hand and introduced herself. "Aubrey Carlson," she said.

England's foremost authority on the American War of Independence. His greatest rival, and one he'd always assumed to be male. Homely. Fat, even. Smelly.

He stammered a few sentences, and tumbled into love.

JULY 5

FELICIA FORGETS HER SCRIPT

FELICIA APPROACHED THIS door with the same enthusiasm she'd approached the eighteen previous doors—that is to say, no enthusiasm at all. So she was surprised when the young woman who answered smiled warmly.

"Can I help you?"

"Oh!" said Felicia. "I wonder if you'd ... if I could tell you ..." She stopped, flustered. She had totally forgotten her script.

"Sure!" said the young woman. "Come in!"

Felicia looked around suspiciously. Surely now she'd be attacked. But the gal sat expectantly, still smiling.

Suddenly, nothing in Felicia's script—in which there were prominent mentions of hellfire and damnation—seemed to matter.

THOSE FEW TREMBLING HOURS

YOU WON'T MAKE it on your own, they said. *You're such a scaredy-cat. Gonna hide under the bed if some kid selling cookies comes to your door?*

But she *was* making it.

She jumped every time there was a *thud* from the upstairs apartment, and there were those few trembling hours when an enormous spider appeared in the bathtub. But she was *fine*.

Really.

When a thunderstorm killed the power, she stumbled to the junk drawer for the flashlight. Dead batteries.

She crawled to the couch, where she willed her heart to calm.

After a while, she embraced the dark.

IT WASN'T ME

NO, MAMA, NO
It wasn't me
This isn't chocolate
That you see
I put my hands
Behind my back
I only took one
Little snack
I don't know what
Is on my nose
And on my face and
On my clothes
It maybe was the
Kitty cat
Who got some crumbs
All over that
I promise I
Will clean my plate
You'll be so proud
Of all I ate
And I won't hide

My yucky peas
Under the napkin
Mama, please
Can I just have
A bite of this
I love you Mama
Here's a kiss
I love you, Mama ...

AIN'T NECESSARY TO PAY

WHEN THE GARDEN'S coming on so quick I can't hardly keep up, I like to leave some vegetables on a table at the end of the driveway. I put a money jar there, but it ain't necessary to pay.

Because when I do the planting, I know the good Lord will bless them plants with fullness. So I just say a prayer for each zucchini and tomato. Every one of 'em.

See that car? Lady just took a coupla vines of tomatoes. Looked around, didn't pay a dime. She don't know that with each one, she'll be swallowin' a prayer.

WITH MY BODY

COLLEEN WATCHED JED as he looked in the mirror for the fiftieth time. He turned from side to side, flexing and posing. His T-shirt was ridiculously tight at the arms and shoulders; he looked like a guy who had tried to squeeze into his eight-year-old son's clothing.

"Do I look bigger this week?" he asked.

"Yes, Jed. You look bigger." She put a hand to the small poochiness at her belly and saw the dimpled softness of her elbows, and remembered the vows they'd said: *With my body I thee worship.*

Jed bent his head and kissed a glistening bicep.

ON THE BUS

DOROTHY RETURNED FROM the Seniors' Color Tour feeling disgruntled. All the attractive men were married; the few widowers were either uncouth or smelly.

A message was on her machine: *Miz Gedart, this is Clarence. Your bus driver. You left your scarf on the bus, that kinda blue one. I knowed it was yours cause I remember you looked nice. Well, when I seen it, I thought, you know. If you wanted, I could bring it over. And maybe a coffee. I noticed you like coffee. Well, anyways.*

Dorothy's hand went to her bare throat, where a pulse was rapidly beating.

JULY 11

DOOFUS

RYAN TRIED EVERYTHING to get Brittany to notice him. He played his ukulele in the company cafeteria; Brittany steered her tittering friends away. He heard that she loved science fiction, so he wore a *Firefly* shirt on casual Friday.

Nothing worked—he eventually gave up. He was subdued, efficient, professional. Brittany gave him a week, then stopped by his desk. "Lunch with me today?"

"Why now?"

"I was waiting for the real Ryan—not that doofus."

"You know what? Maybe not." He looked beyond her, to one of the tittering friends. "What about you? How do you feel about doofuses?"

JULY 12

MIDLIFE CRISIS

WHEN WE WERE newlyweds, whenever Steve saw a sports car, he'd say, "That's my midlife crisis car." Over the years, he shortened it; a fancy little car would whiz by and he'd say, "MCC."

It's been fifty years since we were newlyweds. Last night I looked out at Steve's ten-year-old sedan and said, "You never did get your MCC."

He smiled. "I test drove one, twenty years ago. When we were ... you know. There was something wrong with the wheels."

I raised my eyebrow.

"They only went one direction. *Away.* I told the salesman thanks, but I'd be heading home."

JULY 13

WRECKING BALL

THE PHONE RANG during Leslie's Wii workout. Reluctant to break her rhythm, she stepped off the balance board and grabbed her cell. A wrecking ball swung into her Mii and sent it plunging overboard. "Shoot," Leslie said. She answered the phone.

"Hello?"

"Yeah, this is Rob next door. Tell your husband I got that stuff, but he's gotta come right away."

Leslie's Mii jumped over a log and deftly avoided another wrecking ball. Leslie was panting now.

"Sure thing."

But when Don came home and reminded her that their neighbor's name was Larry, they both sat for a moment, pondering.

LIGHTNING

THE STORM WAS spectacularly violent, so Lillian wasn't surprised when one magnificent *crack* took out the electricity. She couldn't remember the house ever being so totally dark. She urgently missed John, dead seventeen years.

She trembled on the couch, straining to see through the onyx wall in front of her. A lightning flash illuminated the room, and in the corner, she felt sure that she saw Jesus. He was still there with every flash. She stilled her spirit, keeping her eyes on Him.

—*You arranged for the afghan to land just so on the vacuum cleaner, didn't you, Gabriel?*

—*Yep.*

HER MOTHER'S SENSE OF HUMOR

A MIDDLE-AGED woman stood at Deb's door, her arms outstretched.

"I'm here!"

Deb wasn't expecting company. She was braless, in sweats. "Ummm ... who are you?"

"Oh, sweetie, you have your mother's sense of humor. She *told* you I was coming, remember?" The woman pushed her way inside and took a soda from the fridge.

Over the next hour, she amazed Deb with her mother's recent adventures. It was as if she was describing a stranger. "Oh, hey!" she said. "Here's a picture from the rodeo."

The woman in the picture was not Deb's mother.

"So ..." said Deb. "Want another soda?"

POWER WALK

IPOD ... CHECK. PEDOMETER ... check. New jogging shoes ... check.

Joyce set out for a power walk on day one of the new diet. With a jaunty tune in her ear buds, she walked briskly past the pharmacy, the manicurist, the florist.

When she discovered, breathless, that she could no longer sing along to the iPod, she checked the pedometer. Surely it was broken; she shook it and looked again at the number, annoyed. A wild pulse pounded in her throat.

A car slowed down. Joyce's neighbor shouted, "Hey! Wanna ride?"

Thank God. She hopped in, thinking of the cookies back home.

LOOKING CUTE

PEOPLE COMMENT ON my profile picture all the time—the one where I look so cute at Allie's wedding. Here's the story:

I was surprised when she asked me to be a bridesmaid; we weren't that close. "I dunno, Allie," I said. "I'm not a big fan of bridesmaid dresses."

"Oh, please? My cousin's in France, my sister's hugely pregnant, and I don't have anyone else. I *promise* I wouldn't do that to you. Please?"

And Allie was right—no ugly bridesmaid dress. That's me in the middle, between Darth Vader and Princess Leia—the one with the Yoda ears.

SPARK

ONE RANDOM EVENT is the spark ...

A passing semi tossed a stone into Maggie's windshield. *Smack*—dozens of tiny cracks appeared. She cursed and drove to the dealership. Tom strolled out to meet her ... but Tom's not the guy.

One hour, Tom said. Maggie sighed and walked to Starbucks. At the door, she collided with Brian. An explosion of latte.

It's not Brian, either.

A week later, Maggie drove home with her dry-cleaning. When the bag snagged in her car door, she tugged, stumbled, landed gracelessly. Al, walking his pugs nearby, rushed to help. And didn't he have lovely, freckled hands?

SHE TAKES HER PRIZE

IT'S RIDICULOUSLY EASY. A brush of Felicity's hand across a restaurant table, a murmured *excuse me* while waiting in line. Then she walks a hundred steps or so, her pace only slightly quickened, her face barely flushed. When she stops in the first safe place, she takes her prize from her pocket. Her breathing slows; the pink recedes from her cheeks.

Once home, Felicity tosses the item in a drawer full of cell phones, billfolds, glasses.

Sometimes, Felicity opens the drawer when she's looking for some household item. She's always startled by what's there, and she closes the drawer quickly.

RECONNAISSANCE

THE SPACECRAFT WAITED behind the moon for its small reconnaissance team. They'd been given one hour for their mission.

The first to return looked appalled. "People here live after they die, but it's a horrible non-life. They become mindless monsters, intent on murdering their own kind."

The commander, unaware that the agent had been watching television, frowned. "We'll leave as soon as your partner returns, then."

An equipment malfunction delayed the second agent. Eventually they left, without hearing her report: "People here live after they die, a glorious life of eternal bliss."

She'd spent her hour in a well-worn pew.

ON A QUIET BREEZE

EVERY SO OFTEN she catches a whiff of his scent. Leather. Cloves. Clean sweat. Grass. Cedar. She is standing in line at the theater or browsing in the library when the scent teases her, then disappears, an echo of a whisper.

A stranger brushes her shoulder as he leaves the bus, and the scent follows him. She is halfway out of her seat, ready to pursue the man, but then she flushes and sits back down.

At home in her room, the scent wafts in on a quiet breeze. She rests her hand on her heart and speaks his name.

CRAIGSLIST

I WAS SITTING near you at Java Johns. You were with a friend, laughing loudly, and when she left, you continued to laugh while you finished your coffee. Everyone was looking at you, the girl in the funny green hat. You've probably been told about that laugh all your life. You dumped your purse and several items rolled on the floor. You picked them up, but you missed a receipt (feta and shampoo) and a roll of Life Savers. You gave the rest of your danish to a dog outside. Did you see me, the guy in the yellow tie?

IN THE BASSINET

SLEEP WHEN THE baby sleeps, they say, but they don't factor in the jealous toddler sibling.

It was silence that woke Leigh. She looked at the clock; she'd only been asleep five minutes.

"Jilly!" she called.

Toddler footsteps pattered away from newborn Nico's room.

Leigh jumped up and followed, stopping for a peek in the bassinet. Nico was awake, happy, a brown smear on his face. What ... "Jilly!"

The two-year-old appeared at the door. "Emmies, Mama!" She held out a fistful of M&Ms. "Nico have two emmies!"

Expertly, Jilly tipped open Nico's chin and dropped another candy in his mouth.

JUST SO

EVEN THOUGH HER apartment was much smaller than her parents' house, Olivia could breathe more freely within its walls. At home, the omnipresent jumble pressed against her chest, making her feel always on the edge of panic. But here ... here she could place her few belongings *just so.*

Her books—should she arrange them by size or color? Neither arrangement entirely satisfied her until she hit on a brilliant idea. She covered all twenty-three books with jackets fashioned from paper bags and tape, then shelved them from large to small.

Her heart thumped with a feeling very much like love.

10

DENNY HASN'T LOOKED *at me* that *way in ages.* Em swallowed hard. *My elbows are dimpled, there's a spot under my eye, and my heels are calloused. No wonder.*

She turned off the movie and strode to her car. Four hours later she returned, with just enough time for three cookies while waiting for Denny, wide-eyed and slightly panting.

He walked in and laughed, amazed at the dozens of rows of gray-blonde braids circling her scalp. When he saw Em's stricken face, though, he gathered her into his arms. "You're pretty, my Emmy," he whispered. Her neck smelled like honeysuckle.

DIME STORE CASHIER

THERE'S NOT MUCH intellectual stimulation in being a dime store cashier, so I try to analyze people by their purchases. That lady who buys Pepto? Her teenagers give her an ulcer.

Like that.

There's this guy who comes in pretty often, and he buys weird stuff. Turkey jerky. Hearing aid batteries. A squeegee. Every time I think I've got him pegged, he buys something unexpected, like purple candles.

Yesterday, he bought construction paper and crayons. I sure hadn't figured him for a dad. So I was pretty surprised when he brought me that homemade card this morning.

Sweet? Or … stalker?

ANGELA'S BRACELET

WHEN JAMIE WAS three, she had a big sister named Angela. And then Angela was gone. "Where's Angela?" she asked, for a long time, but her parents never said. Angela's things all disappeared. Jamie was angry.

She found Angela's bracelet under a cushion. It had a pretty green stone. She took it and hid it, and tried very hard to keep remembering Angela.

I just wanted to open up a new checking account. When the teller handed me the paperwork, I saw her bracelet, and I couldn't stop shaking. I had a bracelet like that once. I loved you, J-bug.

JULY 28

ELEVATOR ENCOUNTER

WHEN THE YOUNG black man stepped into the elevator, its only other occupant was an elderly white woman with a large handbag, pressing her back into the corner.

He hit the button for the twenty-first floor, then stepped into the other corner. He hitched his pants and looked at the floor; the old woman eyed him suspiciously.

Don't look at me … could be a hidden weapon … wish the elevator would stop … just don't trust those people …

After several seconds the elevator stopped, but it was only the sixteenth floor. The young man hastily stepped out, relief seeping from every pore.

JULY 29—RAIN DAY

SORRY, NO

I WAS A MILE from home, driving in a downpour. When I stopped at the corner, I saw a woman, waving at me. Worried that she was in some kind of trouble, I rolled down the window.

She was 50ish, skinny, wearing a tank top and short shorts. She leaned in; I smelled something sour.

"Hey, got a cigarette?" she said. Rain dripped from her hair.

"Oh! Sorry, I … no. Sorry."

"No biggie." She backed off, and I headed for home.

Take her to the store, you idiot. But when I drove back to look for her, she was gone.

JULY 30

DIDN'T EXPECT THE RAIN

I THINK I SCARED that lady. I figured she wouldn't have a cig, those SUV types don't smoke. And I was dripping all over her nice car and her yellow blouse.

It was funny though, her apologizing to *me*, when I was the one begging for a cigarette and getting her wet. It's not that far to the store—I don't mind walking. Just didn't expect the rain, is all.

I was surprised when I saw her brake lights, though, and she turned around. Was she coming back?

I didn't want to bother her again. I hid behind a tree.

SHOULDN'T HAVE WALKED

DOUG WALKED TO his blind date, but he hadn't counted on the humidity. Half-way there, his shirt was soaked with sweat. Three blocks later, he stepped in dog-doo.

He stood on Cate's porch, scraping his shoe, when she opened the door.

"Doug?"

"Cate!" He held out his hand, still holding a soiled handkerchief. "Nice to meet you. Er … sorry."

"It's … fine." She squinted, sniffed, smoothed her already-perfect hair. At her car, she brushed something invisible from his shirt, then wiped her hand on her slacks.

At dinner, Doug decided not to mention the blob of toothpaste on her silk blouse.

AUGUST

JUST ONE DAY

My MOTHER LEFT us once, fifty years ago, when I was just a baby. Had it happened today, they'd have given her a diagnosis, some pills. But back then … she stood over me in my bassinet and decided it was time to go. She wordlessly handed me to my father and left with just her purse and forty dollars.

That evening, a woman sat beside her on a park bench and lifted an infant to her breast. The baby-smell of talcum and tender sweat wafted toward her, and her breasts, which had been inadequate for me until then, filled with milk.

FIRST DAY

LEVI WORE A camouflage shirt and Batman socks for his first day of kindergarten. I suppose I should have insisted on something more fashion-forward, but his pleading was irresistible.

Miss Roarke stood outside the classroom, chipper in her alphabet sweater, greeting each child by name in that precious elementary teacher voice. I wondered why someone whose name has two R's would choose to teach five-year-olds.

We mothers released our children into her wonderland; most of the moms cried. I spotted Levi through the window, poking Savannah with a paintbrush, and thought, *Am I the only mother who's happy about this?*

DEAREST

PRISCILLA'S STEAMY ROMANCE novels have earned her millions of dollars, millions of fans.

You probably think something ironic is coming. Maybe she's a lonely spinster, or she secretly writes slasher films.

Nope.

Her husband of forty-two years adores her. The picture window in their bedroom looks out at mountains and a placid lake, and he often brings her a little tray, with flowers and some gourmet treat: *foie gras*, chocolate truffles, burrata cheese. He calls her *dearest*, and sweetly rubs her neck between chapters of her latest book.

Priscilla weighs five hundred pounds. She hasn't left the house in years.

AUGUST 4

GONGS, AIR HORNS, MACAWS

GREAT-UNCLE JERRY frightened Rochelle when she was little—his voice always entered the room a long time before he did. She didn't know him well; he only showed up once or twice a year, at Christmas and (with increasing frequency) at funerals.

He'd outlived nearly everyone, holding off death until the age of 93. It fell to Rochelle to empty his apartment. She'd never been there; she imagined gongs, air horns, perhaps macaws.

Instead, she found an encyclopedia with notations in every margin. A collection of hand-tied fishing lures. A flute. In the bedroom, a fat tabby regarded her, silently.

AUGUST 5

ASSISTANT MANAGER

IN HER SECOND week as assistant manager, Wendy got an urgent Sunday night call. Dan was desperate—could she handle the store tomorrow?

This note was on her desk in the morning:

Sry about this, you'll be fine. Funeral Wed., back on Thurs.
Txt if u need me.
Plz check mums in front cooler. Shipment of tulips Tues. p.m. Put in back.
50 carnations dyed blue, high school pep rally Wed. 1:00.
1 pink rose Thurs. a.m., can you hand-deliver to my gal? Address on back.

Wendy sighed. *He has a girlfriend? Shoot.*

Joan Westerbrook
Jordan's Nursing Home, rm. 119

AUGUST 6

COURTING DAY

MANY HANDSOME KNIGHTS approached Princess Liliana on Courting Day, all escorted into her chamber by Duncan, the portly and stumbling squire. They laid their gifts before her, hopeful and eager—and Duncan watched as every knight backed out, stammering and pale, when Liliana lifted her veil to reveal a pinched and poxy face.

Sorry, Lili, thought Duncan. *I miss your smile. Remember playing Goblin Tag? Remember the Haunted Pond?*

She sat on her cushions, downcast, surrounded by hastily abandoned riches, but she looked up when someone tossed a pastry into her lap, plump with golden raisins, and missing one bite.

AUGUST 7

INSPECTOR

MIKE TICKED THE last box on his list. Every left-hand box checked—very satisfying. "Miss Johnston," he said, "there's no sign of insect infestation."

"Oh! You're sure?" She batted her eyes, prettily. "Because I thought I saw ..."

Mike missed the eye-batting as he held out the invoice for her signature. "Yep. No bugs anywhere."

Rebecca brushed his fingers as she took the invoice. "Maybe ... could you check again, in a few weeks?" She flipped her hair.

He pulled his hand away, thinking about the sanitizer in his truck. "Not necessary, ma'am."

Well, she thought ...

Well, he thought ...

That was weird.

AUGUST 8—INTERNATIONAL CAT DAY

CAT LADY

PEOPLE CALL ME a crazy cat lady, but I only have two or three at a time, sometimes four. They find me—usually middle-aged barn cats who just want to spend their last years in peace. How do I know? I just *know.* I can tell when one's coming, and I fix up a bed and a china dish. In a few days, he shows up, purring.

A new one's on the way; I felt her yesterday. Look! Here she comes, bringing me something she caught on the way ... no, that's not it. *Well, hello, little mother. Come on in.*

CONTEST WINNER

THE MINOR LEAGUE team in Nell's city was hugely popular, so she was thrilled when she won WKLT's contest—a date with "the Bobcats' most beloved team member." She hoped it was the swarthy Luis Delveccio.

At the restaurant, the deejay grinned. "Let's meet your date!" he said, and Bobo, the mascot, jumped out from behind a door.

Bobo dipped Nell and planted a plush kiss on her lips. She was humiliated. But when the radio people left, Bobo pulled off his bobcat head. "Sorry," he said. "Not my idea." He was blushing, sweaty.

Nell considered. "Let's eat," she said.

REST AREA

AT THEIR TENTH reunion, Bryan and Liza scratched at each other's spirits. Liza found Brad's buffoonery exasperating, and he found her exceptionally snooty. They headed home in near-silence.

"Should I stop here?" asked Bryan. "Next rest area's 52 miles away."

"I'm fine." But after five minutes, she wished they'd stopped.

An hour later, Liza hustled to the restroom while Bryan set out sandwiches and sodas. They ate at a splintery table; toilet odors floated around their heads.

Six miles from home, Bryan pulled over while Liza slept. He bought violets at a roadside stand, and a quart of plump raspberries.

IN THE MINES

JUSTIN AND CINDY drove through West Virginia on their way to Ohio. Cindy read *Ragtime* aloud as they traveled. She was reading chapter 6 when her voice trailed off, faltered altogether. She closed the book.

"What is it?"

"There's coal in the air. You can smell it."

Justin sniffed.

"My great-grandfather died in the mines. It's why our family moved south. I wasn't expecting coal to be in the *air.*"

They stopped and bought some plastic flowers, then pushed them into the soil just off the highway. On the way home, they found the bouquet again, covered in black dust.

A NEEDLE ON VINYL

JADA LOVES THE scratch of a needle on vinyl, and she's delighted when she finds a radio station that plays *records* from 9 p.m. until midnight. On warm summer evenings, she turns off the noisy air conditioner and opens her third-floor window, listening to KTLW with her eyes closed. She can almost *smell* the past; behind her eyes, she imagines silk stockings, a smoke-filled room.

She's listening to Ella Fitzgerald when she spots the man on the street below. He has stopped walking and he's looking up, searching for … what?

He sees Jada at the window and tips his hat.

AUGUST 13

SHE COULDN'T MISS HIM

DANA CALLED JAMES several times about her project—restoration of an old farmhouse. He had some wrought iron for her; they arranged to meet at a local diner.

She spotted him immediately, slouching over a table, trying to make himself look smaller. He stood to greet her—he was nearly seven feet tall.

Dana understood his discomfort. On a tall day, she barely hit five feet. She held out her hand—well, held it *up*.

Now they're both standing at the altar. It's not *their* wedding—but Dana introduced James to her Amazonian roommate. Life is grand like that, sometimes.

AUGUST 14

MEATLOAF CANDLE

TWENTY-FOUR YEARS of wildly inappropriate gifts bunched together in the attic of Cassie's spirit, a treasure chest of kitsch. Her mother-in-law had a knack for finding exactly the wrong things: a candle that looked like a meatloaf, a concrete goose with a precious bonnet, a book of outhouse photographs.

Why has she never gotten to know *me?* thought Cassie.

She dreaded birthdays.

The sweater was knitted in a sparkly yarn that faded from orange to green. Martha held it to her cheek and smiled. *I love this.* She wrapped it tenderly in tissue and wrote *Cassie* on a gift tag.

PRESSURE

I can't believe he gave me a deadline.

        I can't believe I gave her a deadline.

He knows I don't like to be pressured.

        She hates to be pressured.

I love him. But this …

        I wish I could take it back.

Would he pressure me like this all the time,
if I say yes?

        If I go to her, she'll think I'm pushing
        her for an answer.

I really need to think about this.

      ❣ ❣ ❣

I'm sorry …
        I'm sorry …
        You go.

No, you go.
This is hard.
        This is hard.
I just can't …
        I'll wait forever.
Yes. My answer is yes.

LISTENING TO THE LORD

Maureen woke up on the back porch with a half-eaten drumstick in her hand. *Well, I'll be,* she thought. *I must've walked in my sleep. Lordy!*

The next morning, she woke in the pantry, holding a box of crackers, and decided the Lord was telling her something. *Must be He wants me to walk.* She put on some sturdy shoes and headed down the block on the Lord's business.

Everything looked dandy.

At the corner, she stopped to catch her breath. *Well, I must be wrong. Maybe He just wants me to eat.* She went home and ate four cookies.

CAREER COACH

Twelve minutes late. There's a teenager at my desk, probably job shadowing. I don't see his Careers coach, but I don't mind schooling him.

"In the business world, it's impolite to look at someone else's computer."

He looks up. "In the business world, is it okay to be late?"

Staredown. "Go call your mom to bring you a tie, and learn some manners, kid. *Scoot.*"

He scoots.

Later, I see him wearing a tie, talking with the vice president of sales. He looks like *ohgoodlord the new boss starts today.*

As they walk past, he turns to grin at me.

AUGUST 18

SEMI-FORMAL

[ENTER KEN, WEARING khakis and a plaid shirt.]

Is that what you're wearing?

Yes.

The invitation said 'semi-formal'.

This shirt is new!

[Thoughtful silence.] Do you like this dress? [She turns. Blue chiffon floats, settles.]

You look great. Is that new?

Yes. Just for today. [More silence.] I'm pretty sure the guys will all be wearing ties.

Could be. They'll be uncomfortable.

[More silence. Ken sits down and clicks the remote. Shari squints, then walks out of the room.

She returns in navy slacks and a white blouse.]

Why'd you change?

This looks nicer, I think.

[Perhaps she kisses him.]

AUGUST 19—WORLD PHOTOGRAPHY DAY

PRETTY LITTLE PIPPA

BELINDA WAS DISASSEMBLING a tripod when her phone rang. The voice on the other end was impatient, demanding. "This is Sofia Laine. I want an appointment for an outdoor photo session with my baby," she said. "Very artsy and beautiful. Lots of clothing changes. Can you do that?"

"Yes," said Belinda. Dollar signs danced in her brain. "I certainly can. Are you free on the 23rd? And what is your baby's name, please?"

"Pippa."

On the 23ʳᵈ, Belinda was ready when Sofia and Pippa entered the studio. Pippa was darling in her pink-and-cream lacy sweater. She was a French bulldog.

JUST FINE 101

CELESTE ENTERED THE library just before closing; she'd spent too long searching for her glasses. A sheen of sweat glistened on her lip.

She walked to the fiction shelves, ignoring the librarian, who looked pointedly at the clock. *What's that author's name? Wrangel ... Wardell ...*

Someone tapped her shoulder. Celeste turned, with *don't rush me* on her tongue, but it wasn't the librarian. A smiling redhead grasped her hand. "Celeste! How *are* you? It's been months!"

"I'm fine," she said. "Just fine. Nice to see you!"

The librarian coughed.

As Celeste left, bookless, she thought, *I have no idea who that was.*

HIGH

WHEN EMILY WAS six, her parents took her to the Grand Canyon. She looked over the edge, gripping her mother's hand, and felt like she was falling.

When she was eight, she rode the Ferris wheel. She didn't want to go up so high, but Sadie teased her. The wheel swayed at the top, and Emily upchucked on Sadie's shoes.

Now she is standing on a high platform, buckled into a harness. She remembers the fear, but when the attendant says *1-2-3*, she steps into the air. The bungee trails behind her, and her white hair whips in the wind.

IT'LL DO YOU GOOD

HOT. SO VERY hot.

Bernice lay on her sheet, sweating, while the fan circulated heavy warm air. She could hear the teenagers next door, splashing and laughing in their pool.

Earlier, her neighbor had called over the fence. "Come and swim, Mrs. Coombs," she had said. "It'll do you good!"

But Bernice had refused. She didn't own a suit, wouldn't be caught dead displaying her wrinkles and varicose veins.

But at 2:00 a.m., Bernice got up and walked across the yard. The gate was unlatched. She pulled her nightgown over her head and slipped silently into the cool, cool water.

AUGUST 23

RHAPSODY

EVA STARTED EVERY day at the piano, still bed-tousled. Peter, awake for hours, closed his book when she sat at the bench. "Which one this morning, dearest?"

Today, Eva picked the Rachmaninoff. She started to play the rhapsody from memory; it was not difficult, and she was still foggy from sleep.

When she reached the tenth measure, with the F-sharps in the treble, the song fled from her. She stared at her hands and started again. Peter stood, put a hand on her shoulder. "Eva?"

But the song was gone. A nest of wasps began to buzz in Eva's head.

AUGUST 24

TO SING AGAIN

MILLIE HADN'T SUNG in years, so she was delighted when she was tapped to join this choir. Once quite the singer, she'd toured Europe in college, where she had the soprano solo in Mendelssohn's *Lobgesang*. Her high G was effortless, and the audiences' praise had sent a rush of heat deep into the vee of her draped black gown.

How Millie mourned those soaring high notes when her aged voice became a mere croak! Yet here she stood, excited, preparing to sing again. The song started:

Worthy is the Lamb ...

Music reverberated off walls of jasper, chalcedony, emerald, and sapphire.

AUGUST 25

BACK TO SCHOOL

IT WAS LATE August, and Nina's classroom was empty, the bulletin boards bare. She stood there with a box of notebooks, happily conjuring up memories of children's voices, when a young woman appeared at the door.

"Hello?" she said.

"Hi! I'm Nina Brooks."

"Nina—oh, the one who retired! I'm Hayley. I've got your classroom. Here ... I found these in the desk." She walked to the desk, handed Nina a little bag.

Nina took it, then looked around, unsure what to do.

"So ..." said Hayley, reddening.

Nina sighed and left, leaving her box on a desk on the way out.

August 26—National Dog Day

PANTING AND DROOLING

CHAR WAS NERVOUS about dogs. She'd found a jogging route almost entirely without dogs; the few she couldn't avoid lived in fenced-in yards, or were window yippers.

So she pulled up short when she saw the new dog. A mastiff, or maybe a dang *Cerberus*.

It was staring at her, panting and drooling. Char started to turn around when she saw the dog's long leash. *Okay, then.* Safety made her brave—she took a step toward the dog, saying *rrrrufff.*

Cerberus was on a leash—but it wasn't tethered. He gave her a happy tongue bath before she finally escaped.

August 27

TWO LIVES

Tricia	Tracy
finishes her laundry and puts soup in the crockpot	spends the day in sweats and snacks on leftover carry-out
on the wall calendar, she highlights 'piano' in blue (Zac) and 'soccer' in green (Lilly)	her iPhone reminds her that tonight is Project Runway
at 2:00, she goes to Baby Jazzercise with Dakota, then has coffee with the moms	at 2:00, she does aerobics, then has a Coke and a cookie
heading inside with groceries, she sees	checking outside for the newspaper,

Tracy at her computer   she sees Tricia with her
and thinks   children and thinks

she's so lucky

AUGUST 28

QUIRKY

ADRIENNE ENJOYS A good book, accompanied by a cinnamon latte and mustard pretzels. She knows the combination is weird. That's perfectly fine—she has no one to please but herself.

Alex enjoys a good book, read while listening to a mix of reggae and opera. He knows the combination is weird. That's perfectly fine—he has no one to please but himself.

This would be a great opportunity to have them meet in some adorable and serendipitous way, for them to fall for each other's quirkiness and read books together forever. They'd be really happy, too.

AUGUST 29

WAIT FOR ME

LEAH SAID SHE needed to think about it and begged me to wait for her answer. On the last night I saw her, she waded into the ocean; it seemed as if she would walk forever.

Eventually she came back, water dripping from her fingertips, and sad, so sad. "Wait for me," she said. The next day she was gone.

I waited. And then she was back. I saw her, crazily, in the supermarket, thumping a watermelon.

"Hey, Leah," I said. "I waited."

She said, "Tony," and rested her forehead on my chest. Her snow-white hair still smelled of lilies.

AUGUST 30

FIRST DAY

ANA STOOD AT the classroom door, holding tightly to her new notebook. The teacher showed her a desk, and Ana stared at her shoes while the other students came in, in noisy twos and threes.

After a while, the teacher walked to the front of the classroom. There was a restless silence. Ana peeked around—everyone looked nervous. That made her feel better, so she straightened her shoulders and listened carefully.

The teacher smiled. Ana didn't trust the smiles of strangers, but this was a kind smile. When she started to talk, Ana could understand *hello,* and *America,* and *welcome.*

August 31

DROUGHT

THERE HADN'T BEEN any rain for a long time, nor any sunshine—just a low, gray sky, as heavy and dead as iron.

Occasionally, small hopeful animals would skitter about. Some would sniff the air and scamper away to lighter places. Some simply died, their tiny bones littering the ground.

When the mist finally came, and then droplets of rain, the land firmly resisted. Little pools and puddles formed. The cracks of parched earth filled with water.

Then, in an exquisite moment of yielding, the landscape softened. The sky lightened. A sprout appeared.

In Lisa's heart, the drought was over.

SEPTEMBER

OLD LETTERS

One of the workers handed Cass a crumbling packet of old letters. "Found this in the wall, ma'am," he said, then returned to the demolition.

Cass started to read. They were love letters from decades ago, signed by a man with the same last name as her own.

The letters were full of *dearest* and *promise* and *eternity*. There were pressed roses, poetry, tear stains. With a snort, Cass tossed them into the workers' dumpster. *Whatever,* she thought. *Fine for you, great-great grandpa.*

But when it was time to leave, Cass ran back and put the letters in her pocket.

NONCONFORMIST

At her new high school, Kimmy wore nondescript jeans and tees for the first few weeks, studying the cliques, deciding where she'd like to fit in. None of them entirely appealed to her.

On Mondays, therefore, she dressed like a jock. Tuesdays, prep. Wednesdays, Goth. Thursdays, nerd. On Fridays, she mixed it up, wearing bits and pieces from the other days with a scarf, a hat, or a pair of wacky socks. She sat with anyone at lunch, choosing a table without asking permission to sit, chatting easily.

She loved her nonconformity—until the cool kids started to copy her.

COSTUME PARTY

It was obvious when Molly entered the party—nobody else was in costume. The talking and laughter died down as everyone turned to stare at her, ridiculous in her silly outfit.

"Oh, didn't I tell you?" said Ruby. "It's not a costume party, after all."

There was an explosion of drunken laughter. Molly walked out, feeling dizzy and ashamed. She couldn't take off the costume; she was wearing almost nothing beneath it.

An unfamiliar guy followed her. "If it makes you feel better," he said, "that costume was *made* for Ruby."

Molly snickered; she was dressed as a giant dog.

SEPTEMBER 4

LUNCH WITH NANA

LAST MONTH, MY forty-five year old Nana wore cutoffs and a tube top to lunch. At the diner, she flirted with the waiter and smacked his butt. I slumped down and snarfed my fries.

So today, she picks me up with her hair in a bun. She's wearing slacks, a blue blouse. At the café, she's quiet, tugging at sleeves that hide her tattoos. This time, I'm not embarrassed by Nana—but she's clearly miserable.

Back at my house, she takes my hand. "Which Nana should pick you up next time?" she asks.

No matter how I answer, someone loses.

SEPTEMBER 5 — INTERNATIONAL DAY OF CHARITY

COVERING THE SCARS

THE FIRE WAS no one's fault—a tragic accident—but Meg lived in long sleeves and turtlenecks, covering the scars.

"They're really not bad, Meg," said her sister.

Meg tugged at her sleeves.

She saved her tips for years, working extra shifts so that one day she could afford the plastic surgeon's fee. The day she made the withdrawal at the bank, she saw an ad in a magazine: little brown children with beautiful black eyes and shocking cleft palates.

She sent a check in the mail, then went out and bought a tank top. She felt clean, pure, free.

SEPTEMBER 6 — READ A BOOK DAY

BOOK CLUB

JULIA SURVEYED THE book club. "So," she said. "Why did Elspeth hide the picture? Anyone?" A rush of conversation filled the room. *It was because Roderick couldn't … She thought it belonged …*

No, thought Margery. It wasn't that *at all*. You've got it *wrong*. She opened her mouth to speak, but something inside twisted. These women all seemed so *sure*. She slid her trembling hands under her thighs.

A voice broke through the babble. "Margery? We haven't heard from you. What do you think?"

"Oh!" she said. "She hid it ... she hid it ..." Heat rushed to her temples. "I don't know."

SEPTEMBER 7

GLOVE COMPARTMENT

ROTATING LIGHTS IN her rearview mirror surprised Zoe just as she merged onto the freeway. She looked immediately at the speedometer—not speeding. She tugged her shoulder belt and adjusted both mirrors. The police car was quite close now. Biting her lip, she glanced over at the glove compartment. Surely he would ask for paperwork.

Could her taillight be out?

She edged toward the shoulder, planning what she would say.

The patrol car sped past, and Zoe drew a deep breath. No danger now that anyone would see the pistol, poorly hidden under the proof of insurance, waiting for her.

SEPTEMBER 8—WORLD PHYSICAL THERAPY DAY

BACKBEND

VANCE FOUND MARILYN on the floor, reading a magazine with a couch cushion under her head. "What are you doing down there?"

"Well," she said, "I was wondering if I could still do a backbend. Turns out I can't. And then I couldn't get up."

"You okay?"

"Oh, sure. Everything's fine—" She wiggled her toes. "I just can't get up. Come down here with me." A few things popped as Vance lowered himself.

And that's where their daughter Gina found them, the next morning, spooning under an afghan. They'd slept just fine, but they were happy for a hand up.

SEPTEMBER 9

IDEOLOGIES

AT FIFTEEN, KAYCEE changes ideologies like most teenagers change celebrity crushes. This month she has embraced a kind of radical feminism in which every media image she encounters elicits a derisive snort. She spouts phrases like *objectification of women* and *gender disenfranchisement.*

To show her unity with all oppressed women, Kaycee eschews shaving and deodorant. When the other girls snicker at her fuzz, she scowls at them.

Until the new boy wanders into Spanish, blushing to the roots of his bright red hair. "Is this room 117?" he says, and Kaycee grabs a hoodie to cover up her stubbly legs.

SEPTEMBER 10—GOOD NEIGHBOR DAY

JUST LIKE US

"RICK, LOOK," SAID Lindsey. "Someone's moving in next door."

"Hmmm."

"Their kids must be the same ages as ours—there's a crib and a bike. That'll be nice."

Rick joined her at the window. "Is that a loom? I can't believe someone besides you actually weaves. Weird."

"And a kayak! Rick, they're *just like us.* Awesome!"

Lindsey waited a few days, then took a plate of cookies. The door opened slightly to her knock, and she caught a glimpse of blonde hair, glasses, plumpish hips. Just like her. A hand reached out and took the cookies, and the door closed.

SEPTEMBER 11

AUTUMN MORNING

SHE WAS ALREADY into her first period lesson when Jonathan slouched in, late again. "Dude," he said, "some building just got hit by a plane. On purpose."

Jonathan was notoriously unreliable, and she was annoyed by his tardiness. "You must have it wrong. You owe me thirty minutes after school. Get your book and sit down."

Several minutes later, there was a fire drill. Teachers gathered together and whispered about the news, and she realized that Jonathan had been right. For the rest of the day they watched the classroom television, unnaturally silent. She thought about her daughters, miles away.

SEPTEMBER 12

BOBBY GOES FOR A WALK

SHE WAS FOLDING socks when Bobby tapped her leg. "Go for a walk?" he said. She sighed at his eagerness.

"Fine. Get your jacket."

He obediently shrugged into his jacket, and they headed outside. Near the street, she grabbed his arm. "There's a car."

"I saw it!" he said, indignantly.

After a while, she pointed to his shoe. "Tie that, Bobby. You'll trip."

When he'd finished, he said, "Where should we go?"

"It's awfully chilly. You'll catch cold. Let's go home."

Bobby slumped at her side, thinking about what they say: Men marry women like their mothers. *Mother was nicer.*

SEPTEMBER 13

BOUGHT BY ELISABET

MARRYING GEOFFREY WAS intimidating; his mother insisted *she'd* pay for the wedding, horrified that my redneck family would decorate with dandelions or serve barbecue at the reception.

We were unwrapping wedding gifts in our new home—purchased with Elisabet's money—when I opened one with my granny's shaky handwriting. It was a bulky hand-crocheted afghan, purple and green. I looked at our ivory and periwinkle décor and then at Geoffrey, stricken. Granny would have worked for months on this. Elisabet would despise it.

"Give it here," he said. "I'll take care of it."

He draped it on the periwinkle davenport.

SEPTEMBER 14

THERE WAS NOTHING

LORI LEFT THE market with a bag in each hand, wishing she'd bought fewer canned goods.

She was shifting the bags to her shoulders when two people appeared, running and yelling something she couldn't quite hear. Surely they weren't yelling at *her*—she looked back to see what they were running toward, but there was nothing.

A truck barreled around the corner. The driver leaned out, yelling, "Get in! Get in!"

The runners—Lori could see now that they were teens, a boy and a girl—vaulted into the truck bed, and it sped away.

What did I just see?

SCAM

VERNA PHONED HER daughter, babbling with excitement. "It's the most wonderful thing!"

Heather was skeptical; her mother's idea of *wonderful* rarely coincided with her own.

"Anthony told me about a wonderful investment idea!"

"Who's Anthony?"

"Well, I wasn't sure, but his email was very friendly."

"What did you send him? Mom, it's a scam!"

"Don't be so cynical, dear. It's not attractive. I just sent my bank account number. He's going to triple my money!"

Heather spent a week putting holds on her mother's bank accounts.

A month later, Verna got a check—exactly triple her money, with Anthony's signature.

LUCKY FOR HIM

I WAS READING on a park bench when the old man walked up. He nodded at the bench: *mind if I sit?*

I shrugged: *whatever.*

After a moment, he said, "I saw you at the picture show last week. Walking behind Mr. Astaire, making funny faces. *Easter Bonnet.*"

He thought I was Judy Garland.

"How about singing a song for an old man?"

Lucky for him, I love theater. I started singing *You Made Me Love You*; he closed his eyes, listened. When I finished, he opened one eye. "Guess you're not her, after all. You can't sing for beans."

THIS LITTLE LIGHT

WHITNEY DOESN'T MISS the church she left as a teenager. She was dumpy, pimpled, a divergent thinker, and pretty Christian girls there nibbled her spirit to death with their little sharp teeth. She left, married a fellow who found her beautiful, hid her desiccated spirit away.

But now she sings Sunday School songs to her baby and remembers what it was like to have joy down in her heart. To shine her little light. To know that something is deep and wide. She kisses her little boy's neck and thinks that maybe she would like to shine her light again.

CONSIGNMENT SHOP

WHEN THE KID at the counter fumbled beneath his jacket, Nan figured he'd bring out a handful of change. Instead, he produced a pistol. His voice cracking, the kid said *gimme your money.*

Nan smacked his arm, hard, and the gun clattered to the floor near her. The kid looked up, scared. He sniffed, wiped his nose with his hand.

"*Dang,* kid. This is a *consignment shop.* We don't have no kinda money. Get outta here."

He hesitated, and Nan thought for a crazy moment he would ask for his gun. Instead, he turned and ran. His jeans were filthy.

BEAUTIFUL JASMINE

I'M THE PRETTY twin; Jolene's the good one. I use my beauty for gain: men, cars, jewels. People throw such things at a beautiful face, a shapely body.

Frumpy Jolene has a balding husband, a tiny parsonage, constant laughter. She makes me hate everything I own.

We are mirrors for each other's souls. Homely Jolene is *me*—she looks like me, but with the distortions of my character.

I'm not a praying person—that's Jolene's gift. But if I could, I'd pray that just once, Jolene would look in her Jasmine mirror and see the beauty of her own soul.

WHITE HOT

ANITA DROPPED HELPLESSLY into the desert sand, reaching for a shimmering oasis in the distance. The sun beat down in white-hot waves; there was no breeze. She opened her shirt, attempting to cool her skin, but it only prickled with a shallow burn.

I may not survive this, she thought.

Will left church a few minutes after Anita, and found her sitting in the grass, fanning herself. "Honey, is it another—"

"If you say 'power surge' one more time, I swear I will feed your toes to the ducks."

He clamped his lips shut and quickly got into the car.

SEPTEMBER 21—INTERNATIONAL DAY OF PEACE

AN UNFAMILIAR BUZZ

LOLA WOKE WITH power surging through her veins. *What a strange sensation.* She left for her morning jog with an unfamiliar *buzz* in her brain.

She seemed, more than usual, to notice bumper stickers. *Go Cubs,* said one, and Lola smiled. Later that day, the Cubs broke their nine-game losing streak.

Another bumper sticker read *Rescue a Dog Today.* Lola thought about Bingo, her rescued pug. Nationwide, the amount of pet adoptions increased by 23% that day.

And when Lola read *Visualize World Peace,* a general far away put his head in his hands. *What have I done?* he thought.

SEPTEMBER 22

IRRESISTIBLE

THE SCHOOL WAS only seven blocks from Annie's house, so most mornings she walked. On this fall morning, she passed a large pile of leaves in front of Mr. Bukowski's house, pretty sure that it would be wrong to jump in them.

But after school, she couldn't resist. Pulling off her shoes, she hopped into the pile, enjoying their crackle and crunch.

"Hey! You gonna rake those back up?"

Annie turned, embarrassed. "Sorry, Mr. Bukowski."

"Geeze, Mrs. Werner, I thought you was one of them teens."

Annie put her pumps back on and pushed the leaves back into a pile.

SEPTEMBER 23

MEMENTO

LISETTE LICKED HER thumb and wiped a smudge from Cody's cheek. Cody squirmed and turned her head away; Lisette somehow managed to headlock the wriggling toddler while jiggling a whimpering baby on her knee.

"Honestly, Carly, I don't understand you. You'll really regret not having children, I'm telling you. It's so … fulfilling!"

The baby reached up and yanked Lisette's hair.

Carly winced. "I'm sure. We just choose to find fulfillment elsewhere."

Back at home, Carly took out a memento she'd swiped from Lisette's house—a pink pacifier. She held it for a while, waiting for some maternal feeling to bloom.

September 24

SO SLEEPY

Eduardo glanced at his languid bride, feeling hopeful. "I don't suppose you'd like to go—"

"Too sleepy," Neve said. She reached lazily for an apple inches away from her fingertips, but failed to snag it.

"You're always tired, darling. Maybe you should see someone …"

"Piffle. Doc says I'm fine." She yawned.

"He *would*. Did he invite you to go home with him, too?"

"Eduardo. That's *over*." Neve stretched out on the couch and closed her eyes.

He studied her face—silky, pale, as beautiful as ever—and wished that his kisses still had the power to wake one long asleep

September 25

NORMAN MAKES A DECISION

Norman wondered how long his wife would be, thankful for this food court. He bit into his bagel, and his eyes were drawn to a little boy, maybe six or seven, all alone.

Where was this kid's mother? Norman looked around, but he didn't see anyone who looked likely.

The boy was meandering, playing a hand-held game.

Norman looked again—no mother in sight, and now a seedy-looking guy in a denim jacket was checking out the kid.

Norman thought about walking over to him—but what if the kid yelled?

He took his bagel to the other food court.

September 26—Lumberjack Day

TODAY'S PROVERB

Grandpa's always spouting sayings at me. Drives me nuts. Today's proverb was a jab at my flighty unpreparedness.

"If I had eight hours to chop down a tree," he told me, "I'd spend six hours sharpening my axe."

I can't think of anything less fun.

"Grandpa, if I had eight hours to chop down a tree, I'd spend five minutes looking online for a tree guy. *Can you chop down my tree this afternoon?*"

Grandpa slumped away, pouting.

Oops. Some oatmeal cookies would make him happy; I could do *that*. Found the number of a great bakery in two minutes.

September 27

NOTHING BUT TROUBLE

KAREN AND SHELLY stopped talking as Tiff walked haughtily into the room, ignoring them both. No one spoke until Tiff disappeared up the stairs, then Karen sighed.

"She's nothing but trouble. I should have been firmer with her when she was little."

Shelly touched her friend's arm. "I saw her with Max last week. They were …" She blushed.

"Great. Just *great*. The *last* thing I need is for her to get pregnant." Shelly looked toward the stairs. "Tiff! Get down here! Tiff!"

At the top of the stairs, Tiff switched her tail, not in the least bit inclined to obey.

September 28

TUMMY TRIMMER

DELLA SUSPICIOUSLY EYED the Tummy Trimmer. Her choices: *up* over her ample rump or *down* over her generous chest. And she was still shower-damp.

Ten minutes of grunting ensued. Della worked up a fresh sweat—but the black dress looked *fabulous.*

At the reunion, the Trimmer cut painfully into Della's ribs. She surreptitiously yanked it down a few inches.

When she sat with Robyn and Norma, the bottom of the thing flipped up, causing her dress to poke out as if she had a third, sharp breast below her real bosom. Below the third breast, Della's belly pooched out jauntily.

September 29

HONEY

SHE NEVER BOTHERED with the equipment—the veiled hat, the smoker smelling of pine needles. The bees, she said, knew that her hands were gentle and that she was not prone to flailing about while she extracted the waxy, dripping frames.

Shh, now, she said. *Shh.*

She pulled a frame from the box hive and stood very still while the bees swarmed. She could feel a breeze from thousands of minuscule wings.

When the buzzing abated, she set the frame aside, trapping one small bee against her wrist. *I'm sorry,* they said to each other as the stinger sank in.

SEPTEMBER 30—INTERNATIONAL TRANSLATION DAY
NOT SO DIFFERENT

WE WERE ENGAGED after only a month—I hadn't even met Rafael's family. Now the day was here, and I was excited to meet his large Brazilian clan.

"*Mamãe, Papai,*" said Rafael, "this is Pam, my sweetheart."

"Oh, call me Pum," I said. "Everyone in my family does, ever since my baby brother said it that way."

I thought their smiles seemed a little pained, but Rafael's teenaged sister laughed out loud. *Different culture,* I thought, and went to meet the *tias* and *tios.* "Call me Pum!" I insisted, all day.

Until finally Rafael reddened, and whispered in my ear.

OCTOBER

FINALLY, SOMETHING DELICIOUS

THE TRUTH IN Labeling Laws of 2019 have taken all the fun out of eating, thought Caren. Everything seemed to have *something* wrong with it. **Warning: causes cancer in lab animals ... May contribute to obesity and diabetes … Prolonged use may cause dependency.**

She'd stopped eating some of her favorite foods, dismayed by the pictures of diseased organs on their labels.

She sighed and unwrapped a chocolate bar, pausing with reluctance to read the label. *Probably causes gout or leprosy.*

This product was made from cocoa harvested by slave labor.

Thank God, thought Caren. *Finally, something delicious that won't hurt me!*

OCTOBER 2 — WORLD FARM ANIMALS DAY

SMUDGE

CHLOE HELD DACK's hand as her mother stepped out of her car at the farmhouse driveway. It was Mother's first visit.

"Mom, your shoes!" Chanel pumps, buttery and sleek.

"These old things? Don't worry, darling," she said, presenting her cheek to be kissed.

To her credit, Chloe's mother was fine, if wobbly, for the tour of the farm. Back at the house, she held Dack's arm as she slipped one shoe off. She licked her thumb, rubbed at a smudge, and then with a shrug, she licked her thumb again.

Chloe couldn't tell her — that wasn't a smudge of dirt.

OCTOBER 3

CHOPPIN' WOOD

HE APPEARED AT her door, early in the morning. "Got any work, ma'am? Choppin' wood, maybe?"

She did need some wood chopped, and he looked trustworthy. She nodded toward the woodpile.

An hour later, she walked outside with his money. "You want some lemonade? A piece of pie?"

He hesitated, then shrugged. "Yes'm."

In the house, she sat across from him, noticing the sweat on his lip, his firm muscles under pushed-up sleeves. When he looked up, she smiled warmly. Invitingly.

"I wish …" he said.

"You wish …" She reached for his hand.

"I wish … I had a mother like you."

OCTOBER 4

WEIRDLY UNDERSIZED

USUALLY, THE COMPANY sent Jackie to places like Chicago or Boston, but when the opportunity arose to go to Temperance, she grabbed it. She hadn't been to a small town in years. Maybe visiting Temperance would remind her why she left.

Everything there looked weirdly undersized. The MiniMart, the little one-slide playground, the mom-and-pop restaurant. Familiar yet not familiar, the houses with their toy-strewn front yards drew Jackie into a residential neighborhood.

Small. Everything was small, and when Jackie impulsively parked and knocked on one weathered door, she was surprised to see that her father had gotten much smaller, too.

OCTOBER 5 — WORLD TEACHERS' DAY

STUMP THE TEACHER

NO ONE HAD ever beaten Mrs. Capek at 'Stump the Teacher'. Her students tried every day, each certain that he or she had found a question she couldn't answer. After the day's reading, the quiz, the worksheet, she invited them to try.

"Mrs. Capek, what's the square root of 1,894?"

"Approximately 43.5."

"What movie won the Oscar in 1931?"

"Cimarron."

"Who invented the word *positronic*?"

Mrs. Capek hesitated for one second, then said, "Isaac Asimov." She narrowed her eyes at Cheryl, who grinned.

At home, Mrs. Capek triggered a tiny latch in her wrist and quietly recharged her positronic grid.

SHE FELT FIERCE

MIRA LIFTED THE baby from his bassinette and gave the hovering nurse a nod. *We'll be fine.*

The nurse left, and Mira settled the sleeping infant in the crook of her arm. When he sensed her bosom, the baby pursed his lips and made little sucking noises.

Mira's breasts tingled; she laughed out loud. They'd told her for months about this rush of love. She felt fierce, full of possibilities.

Another nurse came in, carrying a chart. She checked the baby's wristband, then adjusted his little cap. "Time for a feeding," she said. "Better hand baby over to Mom, Grandma."

TILLY SMILED

TILLY SLIPPED OFF the gray shroud before entering her workplace with a toothy smile. She was able to keep it off for most of the day, but alone in her office, she gathered the shroud around her hunched shoulders.

During the afternoon meeting, the interminable PowerPoint and the lists of statistics, Tilly draped the shroud around her head, shutting out the monotony of the speaker and substituting a comforting white noise. When addressed, Tilly smiled and dipped into the pool of business platitudes.

At home, she curled up on her bed, completely covered in her ashen veil of blessed nothingness.

TOUCH

LONG LINES BOTHER Hilary, and crowded places, so usually she stays at home, alone. She doesn't have a phobia; rather, it's a gift, she supposes—or a curse. She only has to touch someone—even a brush of their sleeve—and she knows what they're feeling, even starts to feel it herself. It was fun for a while, when she first discovered it. A great way to make it through school. But her relationship with Emerson was ... problematic. And crowds are simply overwhelming. It's easier to sit in her chair, and hug her own arms, and feel ... nothing at all.

ANOTHER VISIT TO MABEL

MABEL BATTED HER eyes at the young policeman.

"Ma'am, we've looked everywhere. There's no suspicious dog. Have a nice night, and be sure to lock your doors."

"Officer, won't you have some tea? I have some lovely cookies …" She tilted her head coquettishly.

"No, ma'am. And Mrs. Brown, please stop calling unless there's a *real* emergency." He touched his cap. "You sleep tight, now."

Mabel turned away with a pout. There had to be something … she found the tin of mouse poison in her pantry and wondered what just a grain or two would taste like in her morning tea.

FIRE FIGHTER

MR. LEWIS SAYS I have to write out what I did to get detention.

Whatever.

Me and Karly were sitting together for the Career Day assembly, and it's totally not our fault that guy said "fire farter" instead of "fire fighter." Like, three times. So we were cracking up, and Ms. Wells sent us to the office.

Mr. Lewis lectured us for like twenty minutes on how some things aren't funny. We were being very respectful and quiet, I promise. Then when he stood up, his chair stuck to his behind, and we lost it.

Some things just *are* funny.

CARICATURE

THE SIGN SAID *Caricatures, $10.00,* and Samantha tugged her friend's arm. "Let's do it, Mackenzie!" she said.

Mackenzie shrugged, and when he said he'd draw them both for $15.00, they perched side by side on a tiny stool. Twenty minutes later, he handed them the finished piece.

Samantha squealed, delighted; her eyes were her best feature, and he'd made them large and luminous.

Mackenzie stared in horror. The caricaturist had captured her beauty: pert nose, full lips. But somehow, he'd also drawn, in a few swift lines, the blackness of her soul. She looked up; the artist winked at her.

OCTOBER 12—UNITED NATIONS SPANISH LANGUAGE DAY

NEW TRICKS

WHEN A SWEET Hispanic family moved in next door, I decided to learn Spanish. Forty isn't too old for new tricks, right?

We communicated just fine—Rosa and Pedro spoke lively, syncopated English. I kept my Spanish lessons a secret—I wanted to surprise Rosa over coffee some day.

But when Rosa's mother visited from Mexico, I decided it was time. I was nervous. Craig and I rang their doorbell. "*Hola!*" I said to Señora Perez. "*Esto es Craig, mi esposa.*" She lifted an eyebrow.

Rosa tittered. "You said Craig is your wife," she said.

Señora Perez eyed him suspiciously.

OCTOBER 13

SWARM

SHE SWALLOWED HARD, then took a deep breath. When she ran her fingers through her hair, they slightly trembled. Clutching her handbag to her side, she entered the room; a swarm of in-laws waited there, poised to sting.

They all seemed so glib and devil-may-care. She opened her mouth a time or two, closed it again, and reached down to check that her purse was still at her feet. Her sisters-in-law laughed at a joke she did not understand.

After a time, she excused herself. In the bathroom, she took a tiny bottle from her purse and swallowed hard, again.

OCTOBER 14

CHIPPING AWAY

JOURNAL, 1892

Papa ordered me away from the dig, told me to sit under my parasol. How surprised he'll be when he learns that I've found some *hadrosaurus* bones. I set my silver ring next to them—when he finds them, he'll know I have claimed them as my own.

PRESENT DAY

Sara works in the museum basement, late at night, alone. She loves the solitude, the *tink* and *sssshh* of her tools. She's chipping away at a Cretaceous specimen when she finds the little ring, next to a rib fragment. *Well, hello,* she thinks. *How did you get here?*

NURTURING

SHELBY IS IN the nursery, recently painted yellow. She rocks in a chair designed for breastfeeding mothers. She will not be breastfeeding, though; some hostile creature in her womb attacks and expels its tiny occupants.

Brad has given up trying to coax Shelby back into life, so he watches television. Sometimes he glances into the yellow room. Shelby rocks, staring out the window.

A hot stone of grief forms in Shelby's throat; she swallows hard, letting the bitter heat settle in her belly. She will nurture it there. This small glowing rock is something that she can finally keep alive.

GOOD THINGS

MELISSA PRIDES HERSELF on giving her children good things to eat. Today's lunch was a salad of mixed greens, with feta, dried cranberries, honeyed pecans. Thinly-sliced baguettes dipped in herbed olive oil completed the meal. Tonight, she'll serve them salmon smoked on a cedar plank, asparagus tips, eggless chocolate cake.

Late at night, once the children are asleep, she'll slip out of the house to gather their meals for tomorrow. She dresses in old clothes, and she tucks disposable gloves into her pocket.

If she's caught—and she's always caught, eventually—she'll just look for another fine restaurant, another dumpster.

SECOND CHANCE

IT's HARD FOR ex-cons like me to get a job. The guy who owns this restaurant took a chance on me, put me in the back, washing dishes. The people out there never see me, never see the prison tats. I don't make much money, but I don't need much.

I haven't missed a day since I started. I'm part of the background, part of what's normal here. I like that.

The bussers come back here, and sometimes the waitresses, when things are really busy. That redhead waitress? She's gonna be my second chance. Gonna do it right this time.

NOT QUITE REAL

IF IT'S RARE, I sell it. Old toys? I have them, rubbed bare from much love. Old clothes? Those too, frail as dust—high hats and silk gloves.

A room in the back has stuff you'll not find in town. It's not quite *real*, if you know what I mean: I can sell you a glimpse of a lost love, the smell of fog at dawn.

What can I get you? A gram of pain for a foe, you say? A pinch of guilt? A smidge of hate?

That I can't do. These things, sad to say, are not rare.

SIX WORDS

INSPIRED BY THE apocryphal story of a writer who penned an entire story in six words, Professor Twilling asked her Creative Writing 101 students to do the same, only with a twist. Write six words that could possibly change the world, she said.

She got predictable results, for the most part. One uninspired literalist wrote *These words could change the world.* Another dewy-eyed romantic submitted *We should all love each other.* One of Professor Twilling's favorites was *Cookies for everyone—America is buying.*

But this one went viral, and the world actually *did* change:

All corpses are equal. Stop fighting.

PROUD GRANDMA

THE WOMAN PUSHING a stroller was half a block ahead of Kirsten. She was probably in her sixties—a proud grandma. Every few feet, the woman would peer into the stroller, murmuring something Kirsten couldn't hear.

Kirsten's steps were quicker than the grandmother's, so she heard what she said while parking the stroller in front of the library. *You'll be fine here, sweetie. I'll just be a few minutes.*

The woman disappeared inside.

Oh, surely not, thought Kirsten. *You wouldn't leave the baby ...* she hurried to the stroller, angry.

There sat a contented fat calico, wearing a white lace bonnet.

OCTOBER 21—APPLE DAY

APPLES

IT STILL SMELLS like apples here, though the mill has been closed for years. Soon it will be gone; the bulldozer is on its way. I lean against a stack of pallets, remembering the air so thick with pressed apples that it clung to my skin, my hair. My childhood was written here, punctuated with apple seeds.

"Sweetheart? Let's go." Bill stands at the door, covered in sunlight.

"Just … one minute."

Mick was seventeen, a summer helper. He grinned at me for weeks, and when he finally pressed me against the pallets for a kiss, his lips tasted of apples.

OCTOBER 22

NOTES FOR MIL VISIT:

1. FIND AWFUL LAMP and clown picture (basement somewhere?), display prominently.
2. Meals: nothing with butter, green vegetables, potatoes, chicken, mayonnaise, berries, bread.
3. Check with Travis—any new food dislikes?
4. Plan meals. Something with beef and carrots, maybe? IDK what else. Geez.
5. Guest room: flowers on nightstand. Nothing yellow or pink. Assortment of reading material—*nothing political.* Top sheet flowered side *down.*
6. Responses to broad hints about wanting grandchildren:
   > Sorry, not yet
   > Sigh, walk away
   > Is that a new hairdo?
7. Plan outing. Ooooh, get ladies from church to take her somewhere? *Yessssss.*
8. Nod, smile, repeat.
9. Let her win at Scrabble. Or … not.

OCTOBER 23

IN THE CLEARING

LEO DELIVERED FROZEN bagels. On this night, he was driving later than usual; he'd had to get his brakes fixed.

2:00 a.m.—Leo had the road to himself when he saw a purplish light in a clearing ahead. Good time to test the brakes. He pulled over, hopped out.

Maybe he was sleepy. He could swear he saw the shimmering figures of dozens of tiny folk. One of them beckoned to him.

He ran back to his truck, and he never told a soul. But now he always looks for the light. If he sees it again, he'll join them.

GREAT WITH FLOWERS

You're looking at my centerpiece. Interesting, isn't it? It's from my wedding. Twelve years ago. Adam begged me to let his mother do the flowers. *She's great with flowers,* he said. What could I say? I gave Velma magazine clippings of arrangements in the absolute palest pink and cream.

You look startled. So was I, when she brought in these plastic bouquets. Pepto-Bismol and Mountain Dew colors, right? And afterwards, she gave me this flowerpot to keep them in. *Forever.*

When we moved, the pot *accidentally* ended up in the dumpster. Lucky me—Velma rescued them. Just in time, too.

HANDKERCHIEF

Shannon borrowed Brandy's handkerchief on Tuesday. On Wednesday, Brandy was dead, a bolt of lightning having literally snatched her from life in the middle of a word. Only hours before, Shannon had sneezed and Brandy said, "Hold on a sec." She'd dumped her purse and Shannon laughed: who carried handkerchiefs, anyway?

Now the handkerchief is on Shannon's dresser, laundered and folded, a pretty *B* embroidered on the corner. Shannon misses her friend, but the handkerchief makes her smile. She thinks about the sweetness of life—nothing more than the scent of lilacs on the breeze, or a whisper, almost heard.

JEOPARDY

Hello?
Hi, Mom, got a minute?
Well, I'm watching Jeopardy …
I got the job! I'll be doing the news on channel 16.
What is 'A Confederacy of Dunces?'
What? Are you listening to me? So Eric and I will have to move …
What is the Black Hole of Calcutta?
Mom! This is important!

Sorry, dear. I heard you. New job, and you're moving.

Yes. And since we're finally going to have some money, we thought we'd start working on a grandbaby for you.

What is 'Mission impossible?'

I fixed centipedes for breakfast. They were delicious.

Who is Julia Child?

click

OCTOBER 27

SHE CHANGED HIS LIFE

AFTER HEIDI TOLD the principal what she saw Jared do, there was an investigation. Eventually, he was expelled.

Heidi spent her senior year surrounded by silence. When she entered a classroom, students glared and scooted their desks away from hers. If she was assigned to a group, they carried on as if she were invisible.

It is ten years later now, and Heidi has moved far away. Last week she ran into Jared—he actually thanked her. "What you did changed my life," he said with a smile.

But why can't she shake the feeling that someone is watching her?

OCTOBER 28

FOUND ON THE WINDSHIELD

I work in a third story office in the building across the street. I see you most mornings, trying to parallel park. Sometimes you give up and park farther down the block, and I see you walking back to your building with your coffee.

I'm not a stalker, I promise—but I'm good at parallel parking. I could give you a lesson, if you want. You're turning the wheel too soon and too hard—but it'd be easier if I show you.

I like coffee, too. If you're game, how about a thumbs up?

I'm waving at you, right now.

OCTOBER 29—NATIONAL CAT DAY

SOPHIE'S SONNET

I HEAR THAT gakking coming from the den
And rush to intervene—you ball of fluff;
Alas!—a hairball's on the rug again.

I love you, cat, but look—enough's enough.
You're picky when selecting what you'll eat:
No salmon, chicken, cheese, nor anything
But Deli-Cat, perhaps a kitty treat,
A centipede, some pretty purple string.
You never sit upon my lap unless
I'm using my computer there. And yet
I find it lovable, I must confess
That you are unlike any other pet.
O Sophie, how my insides turn to mush
Whene'er I hear you make the toilet flush.

OCTOBER 30

A CHANGE OF SEASONS

EVERY YEAR, WHEN a crispness in the air suggested a change of seasons, Gloria felt a tug of blackness in her spirit. Her vision narrowed in autumn—she could only see one day, the anniversary of an act of violence that had colored every day for a dozen years.

On this particular day, a brown leaf flattened itself against Gloria's windshield, and she ducked reflexively, smiling at the silly moment. It occurred to her, as the leaf flew away, that it was the end of October. The day had come and gone, unremembered and uneventful. She felt full of light.

OCTOBER 31—HALLOWEEN

RAW

"LOUIS," SAID AMELIA, "I think our neighbor is a vampire."

"What? That's ridiculous."

"No, really. Think about it. At the barbecue, he showed up late, after dark. He was wearing all black. He ate his steak practically *raw*. And I didn't like how he was staring at my *neck* all night."

Louis shook his head. "You've been reading too many of those books."

"Well, don't forget his accent. Where's he from, anyway? No one talks like that."

Three doors down, Anton paged through a gluten-free cookbook while enjoying his steak tartare. How he loved this century, with its civilized cuisine!

NOVEMBER

RECLUSIVE

NO ONE HAD ever interviewed Margie Graves, despite her dozens of best-selling novels. She was reclusive in the extreme. It was Javier, her trusted assistant, who filled her mansion with beautiful art, screened her calls, notified the press when she had a new book to release.

Her writing was quirky, a little bit weird—she combined almost random characters with odd situations, and somehow made them work.

Javier types a few words into the computer program he invented: toddler, hippie, heist. "Write me a great one, Margie," he says, then sits back and watches the screen fill up with words.

TAMMY GETS IN SHAPE

TAMMY'S DOCTOR SHOOK her head. "You need to lose sixty pounds. Follow this diet …" She handed Tammy a leaflet. "… and walk 5,000 steps a day. Ten flights of stairs, too. See you in six months."

I can do this, thought Tammy. *I'll start with the stairs.* She'd use the upstairs bathroom—that would be four or five flights. She practically bounded up the steps, twice.

Late that afternoon, she thought about the underwear in the dryer, in the basement. Another flight of stairs.

Butch found her down there, reading a magazine from 1994.

UNDER A GLEAMING FULL MOON

HER SHORT STORY came back from the Creative Writing professor full of red marks in the margin, and Andrea's heart sank. *Awkward … unclear … poor word*

114

choice … contrived. She muttered a comment about Dr. Swinton's ugly sweaters, then settled in with her laptop and some coffee.

She made one correction after another, disagreeing with each of the professor's suggestions.

The room felt too warm. Andrea typed *stupid Swinton,* then deleted it.

Next to *under a gleaming full moon,* Swinton had written *cliché.* Andrea replaced it with *under a pestilent darkness.* Swinton would love that.

Nevertheless, thought Andrea, *the moon* was *full.*

NOVEMBER 4

INVISIBLE

IT DOESN'T REALLY matter how Rhonda was granted her wish—she was given three choices, and she chose one day of invisibility. She hoped to catch Silas in a nefarious act.

"I'll be gone all day," she announced, then walked to the door and whispered the words she'd been told.

After a moment of dizziness, she was amazed—and totally invisible. She tiptoed back into the living room, peering at Silas.

He spent the day in his chair, reading, sometimes dozing.

Once, he got up and ate two cold wieners straight from the package, then performed a spectacularly satisfactory belch

NOVEMBER 5

IN THE BACKGROUND

NIKKI'S ENTHUSIASM WAS irresistible. "I found tons of old videotapes, Jess. From high school. Let's watch 'em together, it'll be awesome."

So they sat in Nikki's basement, watching tapes from ten years ago, a bottle of wine between them. Nikki narrated every scene.

Nikki and Jess as Cinderella's stepsisters …

Nikki and Jess, singing duets in choir …

Nikki and Jess, twirling flags in color guard.

Jess searched the background of every tape, though. There was Austin, the prince's father … Austin, second tenor from the left … Austin, on drumline.

Austin, whose basement still had a VCR.

Jess poured another glass of wine.

NOVEMBER 6

JOB INTERVIEW

DAVID CORRIGAN STOOD and shook Crystal's hand. "We'll definitely be in contact with you soon," he said. "We have a few more applicants, but everything here—" he neatened her papers with a tap on his desk, "—seems to be in order. Pleasure meeting you." He indicated the door.

She was a huge disappointment, he thought. *So good on paper, but she couldn't seem to make eye contact. Can't have someone like that working for me.*

Crystal had no idea how to handle the interview—she simply couldn't bear to look at Mr. Corrigan's one long, untrimmed, and glistening nose hair.

NOVEMBER 7

GRANDMA'S COMING

YIKES. I'VE BEEN a mother for three days, and already I'm messing up. Don't worry, little girl. Grandma's coming.

Courtney! What's wrong?
Mom, look at her!
I'm looking at her. She's pink, she's not crying. She's perfectly fine.
Her eyes! They're open!
She's *awake.* Did you think she was going to sleep forever?
No. But I thought she'd be more ... sentient.
I was shopping, dear. Call if there's a real problem.
But what do I do?
You'll figure it out. 'Bye, sweetheart.

So ... I guess we should talk. How's babyhood working for you? You like that green pacifier, I see.

NOVEMBER 8

MARCUS FOR STATE SENATE

WILLIAM MARCUS' CAMPAIGN car bumped into Ava as the crowd was leaving the "Marcus for State Senate" rally. He apologized profusely and insisted on taking her to the ER himself.

She was *fine,* she said, and the doctors agreed—there was bruising, but no real damage.

He took her to a restaurant afterward, and they talked for hours, exchanged numbers. Finally, the sighing waiter convinced them it was time to leave.

"Thanks for your support, Ava," said William. He reached out, grasped her hand.

"About that ... I was *protesting*. You ran over my sign."

I wonder—will he call her?

LITTLE ALIEN

ALANNIS CALLED THE nausea *flu* and attributed her steady weight gain to stress. She simply ignored the calendar. She'd never paid much attention to the calendar, anyway.

The constant fluttering, though—that was harder to deny. Alannis imagined a little alien, domiciled just beneath her navel. Because that was easier to believe than the obvious truth.

An alien it was, then, until she could no longer hide it beneath baggy sweats. Then she began considering possibilities. Romantic possibilities: a basket, a doorbell. Horrible possibilities: a dumpster.

And finally, in a rush of *yes*, came the answer: another woman's empty arms.

AT 2:00 A.M.

INSOMNIA AND HUNGER drove Corrin to the grocery at 2:00 a.m. At her apartment door, wrestling with two bags and a gallon of milk, she twisted the key and felt it bend. Stuck. Her phone was inside.

Not wanting to wake the neighbors with her ridiculous non-emergency, Corrin sighed, plopped down, and opened the chips.

Across the hall, a light appeared under Mr. Abernathy's door. She'd never met him; there were rumors of not-quite-rightness. She took a swig from the gallon.

Mr. Abernathy came out, with a wine glass and a linen napkin. "Here," he whispered, and disappeared back inside.

SINCE 1972

FRANCIE IS SIXTY-TWO, but she still wears T-shirts from her youth—mostly faded mementos of rock concerts. Her only jewelry is a POW bracelet that she's worn on her left wrist since 1972. Occasionally she checks the website; his name is still there.

She had to remove the bracelet last month for a minor surgery. When she awakened, her left arm felt as if it might float up to the ceiling. She asked for the bracelet, wondering as she put it on if the boy whose name she knows so well was at peace when he died.

Francie, I was.

NOVEMBER 12—FANCY RAT & MOUSE DAY

TINY SWEATERS

MY EDITOR HANDED me three photos—three mice in snapped traps, three different houses. Each dead mouse was wearing a tiny sweater.

"You're an investigative reporter—go investigate."

The houses were all in one neighborhood. I talked to several freaked-out residents, then knocked on Mrs. Murphy's door.

"Do you know anything about these, ma'am?"

"Gracious," she said. "I wish they'd use *humane* traps." She gestured toward her counter, where a mouse hotel rustled. "You know. Winters are so *cold* here. I can't release them without something warm …"

She held up a tiny pair of knitting needles, loaded with blue yarn.

NOVEMBER 13

THEY WERE SO KIND

BOTH WRISTS BROKEN (she'd put out her hands to stop a fall, with spectacular lack of success), and now Patricia was home from the clinic—having allowed the cab driver to search her wallet for the fare—wondering how she'd manage even simple chores with two casts, the left one extending all the way to her elbow; the neighbors watched as she struggled with the key and later they came with a plate of food; Patricia hadn't spoken to them before, didn't approve of them, but they were so kind—even helped her into her sweatsuit, shyly averting their eyes.

NOVEMBER 14

IT LOOKED LIKE FUN

JESSICA TOSSED A glossy pamphlet on Nicole's desk. "This is where Diana and I are going. Please come with us? We'll have a blast, I promise."

She studied the brochure, for a small coastal resort. It *did* look fun.

"I can't."

"But why?"

"I'm just … I can't. I hope you have a great time, though."

Nicole took her vacation at her parents' house. When she saw pictures of Jessica and Diana on her computer, she looked over at her parents with their pursed lips, ever-alert to the distressing possibility of joy. Defiantly, she unbuttoned the top button of her blouse.

NOVEMBER 15—I LOVE TO WRITE DAY

ALWAYS HOPING

THERE'S THIS STORY Carla's always intended to write: a youngish man named Jack sits in a booth in a diner, always ordering the same thing. He's an intense guy, preoccupied with his notebook full of drawings of dragons.

His waitress is fat, sweet-natured Chenille. She gives Jack his plain hamburger and Coke-no-ice with a big smile, always hoping that Jack will look up and see how she longs for him.

Carla thinks of these characters often. She feels sorry for Chenille, who is one of those perpetually hopeful, jolly girls—because she's pretty sure Jack will never look up.

NOVEMBER 16

THE GIRL YOU DIDN'T DATE

AT NIGHT, WHEN the house is quiet, you pull out the yearbook and look at the picture of the girl you didn't date.

You remember her voice—a little raspy, like she was getting over a cold. Her front tooth was slightly chipped, and there was a small mocha birthmark on her upper arm.

You think about the time you almost asked her to a movie, and how that would have led to a kiss. She would have loved you.

You can stop; she's fine. She was in your building yesterday, and you didn't even recognize her. Let her go.

NOVEMBER 17

THE GIRL ON HIS BUS

LEROY WAS UNEASY about the girl on his bus. He glanced at her in the mirror— no more than fifteen, wearing almost nothing. Her eye was bruised.

He stopped twenty miles from her destination, the heart of the city. "Miss," he said, "you gotta get off."

"What?" She looked outside, frantic. "But I have to go—"

"Sorry. This bus don't go there." Leroy took out his wallet and gave her forty bucks. "Git along now."

He practically pushed her off the bus. She stood on the sidewalk, trembling. Leroy pointed to the mission across the street. "Git along," he repeated.

NOVEMBER 18—GEOGRAPHIC INFORMATION SYSTEM DAY

GARMIN INSISTED

"IN .3 MILES, TURN left on Eddy Street."

Karla looked at Garmin. "Are you sure?" she asked. "That's not what Ray said."

Garmin insisted. "Turn left on Eddy Street."

"Fine," said Karla.

Nothing on Eddy Street looked familiar. Karla glanced over; Garmin was indicating a right turn in 2.4 miles. That seemed totally wrong.

Eddy Street became a traffic circle—one that had definitely not been there last time.

"Recalculating."

"Shut up."

"Recalculating."

"Shut up!"

Karla drove around the traffic circle twice and found herself pointed toward home. The heck with it. She didn't need that three-hole punch, after all.

NOVEMBER 19

SOMETIMES

PRINCESS SHOWED UP at the hospital just before her third birthday, a victim of unspeakable violence at her parents' hands. When she recovered, she was adopted by one of her nurses, who spent years loving the pain away.

Princess doesn't remember the people who nearly killed her, but there is a dark and noisy room in her spirit that she keeps securely locked. Sometimes she reaches for Brenda's hand. Sometimes Brenda holds it until Princess's heart remembers how to beat.

Princess doesn't mind when children tease her about her scars. They are the places where Brenda knit her back together.

THE ARCHITECT'S WILL

THE LAWYERS WERE baffled by famed architect Ruth Godwin's will. Her fortune had been hidden. The right person would find it.

A treasure hunt followed. Every corner of every Godwin building—houses, churches, libraries—was searched by fortune hunters eager to be the "right person." Nothing was found.

In the Godwin Progressive Schoolhouse, eight-year-old Paige slammed the storeroom door and rolled under the shelves, panting. Footsteps pounded past, and angry voices. She saw a little brass sign at floor level, with words in an interesting code. *I wonder what that says.*

It took her seventeen days—but she got it.

EAST

CALLIE SEES THE hitchhiker in the distance and thinks, *I shouldn't.* But she stops, and he climbs in the car.

"Where you headed?" she says.

"East." He nods in that direction. "Mind if I smoke?"

"Um. I'd rather you didn't."

He puts the cigarettes in his pocket, but after a few miles, he takes them out again. "You'd *rather* I didn't, but kin I smoke?"

Callie shrugs. "Oh. I guess."

He rolls down the window, flicks ashes outside. When he finishes his cigarette, he lights another, then a third.

It's cold with the window down, but Callie keeps driving east.

NOVEMBER, 1963

THE DAY HE died, I was eight years old. My teacher cried. I hadn't realized such a frightening thing was possible.

Later, on the playground, children laughed and chanted. My teacher made us come inside and put our heads down. She walked the entire classroom, gently chastising those who'd laughed, reminding us of his two little children.

When she passed my desk, she touched my shoulder.

I'm still haunted by that touch.

Did she think I was one of the laughing children? Did she touch every child? And worst of all—I was only eight. I think, maybe, I laughed.

UNINVITED GUEST

THE FAMILY HAD just settled around the Thanksgiving table where they heard the doorbell. "I'll get it," said Walter. He opened the door and gaped at the man standing on his porch. "Oh, my God!"

"Yep," the man said. "How you doin', Walt?" He leaned into the doorway and waved at the astonished family. "Hey, everyone. Am I too late?"

"Uh, no," said Walter. We were just about to pray. *Weren't* we?"

The family all nodded. Libby scooted over, and Lorraine went to get another plate.

"So," said Walter. "We're, uh, thankful for …"

"You're welcome!" said the man. "Let's eat!"

FIRST THANKSGIVING WITHOUT THEM

MY PARENTS DIED, as predictably as a cliché, within weeks of each other. The hosting duties for this first Thanksgiving without them have fallen to me.

I debate the proper approach. Forced giddiness? Glum reminiscing? Finally I decide to ignore every family tradition altogether.

It mostly works.

During dessert, Gwennie's new husband speaks up, mouth full and eyes wide. It is only his second Thanksgiving with us. "Holy Schmidtt," he says. "This tart thingamabob is *way* better than that crappy pie we had last year."

Mom's pumpkin pie *was* terrible. No one makes eye contact, but Uncle Jim silently nods.

JUST ONCE

THERE'S SOMETHIN' ABOUT a 'lectric organ playin' 'Jes As I Am' that practically yanks sinners to th' altar. Good preachin' helps, too, an' I been blessed with that gift, praise God. I had 'bout a dozen folks up there tonight, weepin' and wailin'.

I believes every word I preaches, too, not like some a them travelin' evangelists who's jes in it fer the money and the wimmen. I rejoices fer every lost sheep that's brought back into th' fold.

But jes' once—it'd be nice t' hear God speak to *me*. Lord, Lord … I'd even take a still, small voice.

SHE DID NOT WEEP

ALLISON'S HUSBAND DIED last month. They'd been married twenty-seven years, years in which Allison perfected the dodge, the block, the lockout. She did not weep at his funeral.

Allison is moving to a smaller place now; the walls of this house are saturated with the echoes of her husband's fists.

She is going through a desk when she finds some handwritten music from years ago, before the music was smacked out of her soul. She had titled it "Serendipity," and it was rich with syncopation and unexpected intervals.

Allison holds the paper to her heart and whispers, "Hello, old friend."

ON MRS. NOVAC'S DESK

KATIE FLED TO the art room in despair; she'd failed her geometry final.

Mrs. Novac was cleaning paintbrushes. "Perhaps you can retake it?"

"Mr. Dunn says no."

"I'll speak to him. Come back after school."

When Katie returned, the test was on one of the paint-splotched desks. She tackled the lengthy proof; it was no clearer than it had been earlier. Mrs. Novac painted in the back of the room.

"Katie, could you get that rag on my desk?"

And there was the answer key.

Katie looked up; Mrs. Novac lifted her chin toward the desk, then turned her back.

NIGHT FLIGHT

IT WAS A NIGHT flight back home, and Brooke planned to use it to compose the note they'd find with her body. A bottle of pills whispered to her from her carryon bag.

But the woman in 13D was a first-time flyer, a nervous chatterer. Brooke had to show her the overhead light, the air blower, the seat tray. She heard about the woman's grandson's first steps, her husband's shingles.

When they landed, 13D touched Brooke's cheek. "Bless you, dear," she said. "You've been very kind. I couldn't have managed without you."

The whispers from her bag stilled, for now.

November 29

SNAKE TO WOMAN

Go ahead—it's tasty—
Feel its juices on your chin:
Eat.
This fig—you like it?
Here's another one.
Again.

Don't you love the sweetness?
Sure, it's sticky—we don't care.
More?
Don't think—enjoy it.
If you want to, we can
Share.

Adam isn't here—you're free.
No regrets. Believe in me.

Just don't look inside, girl.
Some things you don't need to know.
Hey!
… Yes, that's a wasp there.
Just ignore it. Let it
Go …

Come—eat your fill. There's plenty,
Just as juicy, just as sweet.
Mine.
My dear, you're mine now.
Such a luscious little
Treat.

SHE PLANNED TO KNIT

DOREEN WAS EXCITED to house-sit for three weeks. Her friends had a lovely house, and Doreen's tasks would be few: fetch the mail and newspapers, keep the dogs happy. Three walks a day, kibble and water, the occasional scratch behind the ears.

She planned to knit an afghan.

The bulldogs were obese and stinky, and they snorted. And farted. They yipped at Doreen's knitting needles, apparently thinking they were some sort of weapon. They pranced at her feet for attention and barked at invisible squirrels. They thought they were lap dogs. They farted some more.

Only twenty days to go.

DECEMBER

WITHOUT HIM

EILEEN TOOK RONALD's hand. "I think you should take the job."

"Are you sure?"

"It's only three months apart. It'll be over before we know it."

At first, it was hard. Eileen made too much food, and she couldn't sleep without Ronald's snoring. But after a while, she thrived on her own. She started to paint again. She read long novels, painted her toenails, went to a sushi restaurant. For three whole days, she didn't even think of him.

She didn't realize it was there—but his return filled, with a rush of warmth, an enormous hole in her heart.

HAPPY BIRTHDAY, OWEN

GRANDMA SALLY AND Nana Paula met at little Owen's house for his first birthday. They hadn't been together since his birth.

Nana grabbed the little boy and put some new, sturdy white shoes on his feet. "Babies need shoes," she pronounced. Later, Grandma wrestled them off. "He's not walking yet," she said. "Shoes are silly."

Nana gave Owen numerous expensive toys, professionally wrapped.

Grandma held out a little wooden truck, handmade.

And when Owen said *nana*, didn't Paula look triumphant? But Grandma Sally claimed the victory. "I taught him that word," she said, and took a banana from her bag.

LOST

KAYLEE DIDN'T HEAR the people calling for her, didn't see the helicopters. She curled up under one of the trees and cried.

126

When she was done crying, she lifted her head from her arms. A man was there, smiling. "Kaylee, I can take you home." There was something sparkly about him.

"My teacher says only go with someone in a uniform." She wiped her eyes, then looked at the man again. He *did* have a uniform, with a badge and a cap.

Back at home, in her mother's arms, she tried to describe him. "He was really nice," she said.

MOST LIKELY

THE YEARBOOK COMMITTEE didn't have any trouble coming up with *Cutest Couple, Biggest Teacher's Pet,* and *Best Dresser.* When they came to *Most Likely to Succeed,* Sabrina squealed. "Oh my god, let's pick Mariah."

Mariah—fat, pimpled, shy to the point of near-muteness. They gave her a full-page spread, deftly bypassing their advisor.

And they were stunned, the day after yearbooks came out, when Mariah walked heavily into the yearbook room. "I *will* succeed," she said, then lumbered out the door.

At their ten-year reunion, Sabrina sat at the table of nametags, hoping and not hoping that Mariah would come.

SAFE SCHOOL

KRISTINA IS SO dumb she doesn't even realize when I say, "Pretty shirt, Kristina," I'm totally making fun of her. She just smiles and says *thanks.*

But Mrs. Malloy squints and shoots me a warning look.

"What?" I say. "I'm just *saying.*"

This is a "safe school" now. No bullying allowed. What's Malloy going to write me up for? Excessive complimenting?

I tell Kristina her hair is nice, her backpack is cool. Malloy says, "That's *enough,* Amber."

Kristina's starting to catch on. Duh.

In the hall after math, Tiffany swishes her blonde hair at me. "Nice *shoes,* Amber," she says.

INSOMNIA

DESPERATE TO GET some sleep, I finally buy the pills I've seen advertised on TV. I settle into bed; my brain instantly fills up with all the old worries and a new one—will a huge green moth fly into my bedroom now?

It takes hours to fall asleep, but when I awake, I feel amazingly rested. I check my phone for messages; wonderfully, my worrying has finally paid off. My son has dropped his strident girlfriend, my daughter has decided to go back to college, and there are toadstools growing out of my fingers.

Wait. What?

Darnitall. Still asleep.

OBSTACLE COURSE

IT'S A GREAT room. There are colorful balls and fun-looking pieces of exercise equipment—large rubber bands and punching balloons in happy primary colors. A small stairway and a ramp look like an obstacle course for adventurous toddlers.

But look again—more ominous pieces of equipment are here: parallel bars, wheelchairs, harnesses. There is a tang of bleach and sweat in the air. No one is having fun here.

A therapist tosses one of the jolly balls to an old man who says, *"oof,"* as it lands in his lap. Three seconds later, he lifts his hands to catch it.

IN BECCA'S JOURNAL

THE MOVING VAN pulled in across the street, and Becca watched through her window with vague curiosity slowly turning to wonder. That hutch, that bed— she riffled through the pages of her journal; there they were, described in notes for a romance novel-in-progress.

And … yes, there *he* was, shaggy hair and faded jeans, carrying a stack of books. Becca squinted and saw *her,* all raven tresses and pale skin. Straight out of her journal. Looking just like Becca—well, like Becca's more beautiful, more desirable sister.

Did I …? I wonder …

Becca grabbed a pencil, and started to erase *raven tresses.*

CLOUDS

BRENNA WAS CUTTING lilacs when she saw the strange cloud formation. Knowing the ephemeral nature of cloud formations, she took out her phone and snapped a few pictures. Sure enough, within just a few seconds they'd shifted; she laughed and continued snipping lilacs.

Back in the house, she pulled up the pictures. She hadn't been mistaken—the clouds had, for a moment, looked like the smiling face of Jesus.

Her first smirking thought: *Just like Jesus, to show up, then disappear.*

But more and more often now, she looks at the pictures and thinks: *Just like Jesus—to show up.*

HOMELY

LOIS WAS A plump, homely girl who grew up to become a plump, homely woman. She moved away from her hometown right after high school, to escape the pretty girls who'd tormented her for years.

And then she came back. "I need you here," said her mother. Her father was ill, her mother emotionally fragile.

Lois dreaded seeing the pretty girls who'd stayed in town, started families. She saw Candi first, at the deli. Candi hugged her. "I was horrible in school," she said. "Can you ever forgive me?"

Lois considered, then held her grudge even tighter to her chest.

IN THE HALLWAY

JUDY STEPPED ON a pencil in the hallway and her ankle wobbled. She lurched forward several steps, dropping her students' papers and windmilling her arms before she was finally able to stand, one hand against the trophy case.

She looked around, mortified. The halls were empty except for Dino, who smirked.

I shouldna been in the hall. I was skipping math, grabbing a smoke. It was pretty funny when Mrs. Cabot tripped like that. It ain't cool, but I laughed. But it was awesome, the way she stood up and smoothed her skirt. Kinda dignified. She mighta been pretty once.

KITTENS

LINDA WAS UNEASY about the new PTA policy of having meetings at members' houses. She rang Beth's doorbell, then nervously peered inside.

"You okay?" said Beth.

"I'm … worried about cats. *Kittens,* actually. Crazy phobia, huh?"

"No kittens here. C'mon in!" Relieved, Linda stepped inside.

Kim chimed in from the couch. "My house next month, Linda. No kittens."

Two months later, Linda hosted the meeting. She opened her door for the first arrivals; Kim paled, grabbing Susan's arm.

"What … oh, sorry. I'll put Fluffy away." Linda took the large, hairy spider from her shoulder and plopped it into a nearby tank.

GRAFFITI ARTIST

THE ARTIST CROUCHES in darkness, waiting for the right moment. Not yet—a woman is walking her boxer; there are cars in the street. Still too early.

Four cans of spray paint stolen from the hardware store are the artist's tools; a brick wall will be the canvas.

Finally it's time. Hands shake and spray the cans in a dance of shape and color.

Graffiti finished, the artist runs home, sneaks in a bedroom window.

"Did you sleep well, sweetheart? Rosita, please bring Alexis some tea."
Alexis hides her hands in her lap, picking at the paint on her fingernail.

NEWFANGLED

BARBARA ISN'T SURE that she likes all the new things the young folks are using these days. They make life easier, she supposes—she'll admit they save time on everyday chores and make communication so much better. But she longs for simpler days, when honest hard work left a person good and tired at the end of the day. When people talked with each other face to face. Sometimes she wishes she'd been born 100 years earlier.

"And now what's this?" she says at the strange device at her daughter's house.

"It's called a sewing machine, mother, and it's wonderful!"

SHE FOUND HIM

THEY LEFT AT the same time—Carol in the car, to buy onions and cocoa, and Greg on foot, to get a battery at the nearby drugstore. The sky was low and gray.

Carol spent only five minutes finding her items, but when she left the market, there was a steady rain. She looked off toward the drugstore. *Greg's walking.*

By the time she started her car, the rain was driving hard. She took off, peering left and right. It was hard to see, but she found him—his bald spot shining through the sheets of rain.

She kept driving.

HYPERBOLE

EVERYTHING ABOUT THEM was hyperbole. They'd fallen—literally—at first sight, both so smitten that they'd stumbled into walls. He was a country fellow who dizzied near skyscrapers; she was a city girl who yelped at spiders. When they met at the funeral (his great-aunt, her grandmother's college roommate), they just *knew.*

They met the next day at his cabin. She dressed as she imagined a country girl would: white canvas shoes, pressed jeans, a jaunty scarf. The shoes quickly muddied on the wooded path where they walked, holding hands. A grasshopper landed on her arm. She'd never been happier.

ARSONIST

THERE'D BEEN A series of small arsons in the village: a doghouse, a dumpster, a storage shed. Esther Logan thought *hoodlums* when she passed the burned shed on her way to work.

But Esther wasn't thinking about vandalism as she graded her 4th graders' homework on similes.

My cat is as soft as a kitten.

Esther sighed and took another paper.

I was as angrey as a dragen.

Esther thought, *are dragons angry?* and read on.

Fire is as pretty as a pretty gril.

Jace Gibbons. She pictured Jace's perpetual scowl, and a rush of heat flickered at her neck.

PROMISES

AUDREY TOOK OFF her rubber-soled shoes and rubbed her feet, groaning. When the ache subsided, she pulled all of her tips out of her pockets and spread them on the table.

She gathered the coins into a Tupperware container. The bills went into envelopes marked *Rent, Bills, Groceries*. She took a fiver out of the *Groceries* envelope, thinking of the liquor store. She put it back.

Two pieces of paper remained: a lottery ticket and a gospel tract.

She snorted; both promised her something she'd never been able to find.

Sighing, Audrey tossed one of the papers into the trash.

KIDDIE KARNIVAL

I'M EATING A corndog, watching my grandson at the Kiddie Karnival. A mother lifts a little girl wearing a blue tutu into the bumblebee ride. The girl is somber, wide-eyed.

When the bumblebees start their leisurely rotation, she whitens, then gradually relaxes. But the silly bees rise a few feet in the air, and she begins to cry.

The little ride finally stops; she's sobbing, and her mother rushes in to fetch her. I think, *Good, Mommy will comfort her*, but the woman hauls her out by one arm. "Stop it! Stop crying!" she hisses. "No ice cream for you!"

WEALTHY

HE WAS CHOPPING wood in a Mexican village, but I recognized him immediately: famous millionaire, mysteriously missing.

He recognized me, too—I'd interviewed him once, when I was famous. Before the fall.

He put down his axe, nodded. "C'mon in," he said. His *casa* was smaller than one of the bathrooms in his previous mansion.

He'd sold it all. Most of it was here in this village—a school, a hospital, several home industries.

"Do you miss it?"

"No," he said. "This is my mansion now. These are my people."

And now they are my people, too. *Gracias a Dios.*

SCHNITZEL

SABINE CLICKED HER ballpoint pen several times. Only eight squares to go, all in the upper right corner. A prickling of anxiety settled behind her eyes.

18-across: *Veal dish.* Sabine had 'SC--', but SCALLOPINI didn't work; too many letters. She tried another angle. 7-down: *Stuck,* seven letters, beginning with 'A'. She clenched and unclenched her left hand, thinking hard. She was so close.

ADHERED! That put an 'H' in 18-across. SCHNITZEL, and that made 14-down SELES.

That was it, then — the entire puzzle done, *no mistakes,* entirely in ink.

Sabine grabbed her startled husband and danced him around the room.

NEW NEIGHBORS

"HEY, MONA," SAID Ralph. "Who just moved into that brick house?"

"Hmmm. Mc-somethings. Why?"

"Because they're *here*, with a present." Ralph pushed himself out of his La-Z-Boy.

"Oh, lordy. Stall them!" Mona rushed to the den and began frantically searching. When she found a bottle of cologne — a present from some student, years ago — she shoved it into a gift bag, ignoring the cloying odor surrounding the bottle.

"Hi!" Mona thrust the bag into her startled visitor's hand. "Merry Christmas!"

Stacy McCord flinched. "Sorry, we thought June and Hank lived here. We're taking this ..." Her voice faltered, and she sneezed.

ZING

WILMA STARTED HER fruitcake in October, with something like glee. This year she had a secret ingredient that would give it extra zing.

For weeks, she marinated the cake, humming a jaunty tune and eagerly anticipating December, when she'd give it to crabby Mr. Wallender. If anyone needed Christmas spirit, it was Mr. Wallender, who refused to acknowledge that his odious dog had destroyed her roses. A fruitcake would be the perfect peace offering.

When she delivered it, he looked startled, but at her urging, he took a bite. Satisfied, Wilma went home and waited for the sound of sirens.

DECEMBER 24—CHRISTMAS EVE

SLEEPY

MADDIE WAS TOO excited to sleep. She could hear her parents moving around downstairs, and with every *bump* or *clink,* she wished they'd go to bed. The morning would never come while they were awake.

Then it was quiet for a long time. Maddie couldn't hear the television or any kitchen noises. She was getting very sleepy—her foot jerked and she sat up, a little spot of drool on her pillow. Then she heard a small sound downstairs.

She tiptoed to the railing.

Daddy looked at Maddie, the pinwheel cookie that she'd left for Santa halfway to his mouth.

DECEMBER 25—CHRISTMAS DAY

VERY SPECIAL

WHILE THE TURKEY and stuffing were heavy in the bellies of the Andersen clan, Metta clapped her hands and said, "Listen! Dad and I have an announcement."

They had decided to loosen the purse strings; there was no sense hanging on at their age. Christmas this year would be "very special."

The Andersen children speculated for weeks. College funds … SUVS … European vacations. Their parents could easily afford to give those.

Weren't they surprised, then, when they opened their manila envelopes? Deeds to a family plot, and a picture of the "Andersen" obelisk at Whispering Pines. The carving was exceptionally fine.

DECEMBER 26

TWO KINGDOMS

SHE STANDS AT the gates to the kingdom and reads the sign there:

PLEASE COME IN.
EVERYTHING HERE IS FREE.
WE WANT YOU TO LOVE US.
IF YOU DO NOT, WE WILL
TORMENT YOU FOREVER

She looks through the gates, where the kingdom is beautiful and abundant. She turns—there is another gate, another kingdom, another sign.

PLEASE COME IN.
EVERYTHING HERE IS FREE.
WE WANT YOU TO LOVE US.
EVEN IF YOU DO NOT, WE WILL
LOVE YOU FOREVER

She looks through the gates, where the kingdom is beautiful and abundant. Which kingdom do you think she will choose?

DECEMBER 27

JUST A GLIMPSE

JUST AS SHE'S waking, Cori always sees a glimpse of someone else's future happiness. It's usually someone she doesn't know, but sometimes she's lucky enough to see her neighbor with a new puppy (he buys it a month later) or her cousin, traveling to Rome (she'll go in 2018).

This morning, she sees a short, mustachioed man standing in a church, weeping for joy. She thinks, *I wish he was looking at me.* She'll spend the next year looking for him, but she won't find him.

He's a thousand miles away. But don't worry, Cori—he's looking for you, too.

DECEMBER 28

STUCK

HEY! CHUCK? I'M down here! Thank goodness you're home.

Stop laughing and *help* me!

Well, I went for a walk and forgot my key. This little basement window was the only one open.

I *thought* I could fit.

I dunno, what time is it?

Three hours, then.

It's in my back pocket. Anyway, I wouldn't call 911 to rescue me from breaking into my own house.

Yes, if we had neighbors, I'm sure they'd love to help. After they finished laughing. *Help me!*

I'm not sure. Push, maybe.

No, wait! Pull.

Ow … owwww!

Thanks. Stop laughing.
I need ice cream.

INCREASINGLY STIFLED

ADDISON HAD BEEN trying for half her life to escape her parents' totalitarian rule. She'd tried to leave, more times than she could count, but every attempt was thwarted.

Your place is with us, Addison.
Don't even think about it, Addison.

And so she stayed, feeling increasingly stifled by their unreasonable rules and restrictions.

But now Addison sensed an opportunity. Determined to find her own way, she'd been working on assertiveness and self-confidence. This outing with her parents seemed an ideal time to try them out.

"*Down,* Mama," she said, and she squirmed out of the mother's arms and ran.

TWO LISTS

CHRISTINE STUMBLED INTO the new country by mistake; she simply followed an intriguing path until she found herself in a beautiful new home.

Once there, she looked for a native, to learn their customs. "No problem," said the citizen, and he handed Christine three lists:

Things We Hate.
Things We Ignore.
Things We Don't Do.

Christine was startled. When compliance became too burdensome, she sadly looked for the path to her old country.

Another citizen stopped her, though, and took the lists. Sighing, he gave her three new lists:

Things we Love.
Things We Welcome.
Things that Make Us Dance.

AT PEACE

I FEEL WONDERFUL.

I'm dying.

My doctor said *viral endocarditis.* It's killing me.

My sister spent our childhood making me miserable—I saw her stricken look when I said *just weeks, maybe* and decided to give her absolution. *You can help me,* I said. I withdrew my savings and rented this cottage on the lake.

Cathy and her kids come every afternoon, and I cheat at Uno. They leave me alone in the evening after putting delicious things in my little fridge. In the mornings, I look at the water. I'm at peace with God.

I really hope I'll just

A NOTE FROM JAN

THE SEED FOR this book was planted in my childhood, when my father told me a story about a fishmonger. In this story, the fishmonger, whose shop was on the docks, thought maybe he could sell more fish if he had a sign made, so he went to a sign maker and asked how much this would cost.

"Five dollars for each word," said the sign maker.

The fishmonger was a very thrifty man, and desired to convey the maximum message with the minimum words. After a moment's thought, he said, "Fine. Have the sign say 'Fresh Fish Sold Here.'"

"I can do that," said the sign maker. "That'll be twenty bucks."

But twenty dollars seemed steep to the fishmonger. Surely, he thought, he could make the message shorter still. "Wait! Make the sign say 'Fresh Fish Here.' Everyone knows I'm *selling* the fish—I'm certainly not giving them away."

The sign maker shrugged. "Sure. Fifteen bucks."

Still not happy, the fishmonger thought again. "No, wait. Just put ... 'Fresh Fish.' Because of course I'll be selling them right where the sign is. No need to paint 'Here.'"

"Ten dollars, then," said the sign maker.

But the fishmonger was still thinking. "Well, of course the fish are fresh. I'm certainly not going to sell fish that are going bad. What kind of fishmonger would I be? Just have the sign say 'Fish.'"

The sign maker sighed. "Very well. That'll be five dollars." He held out his hand to the fishmonger, hoping to seal the deal before the other man did any more thinking.

The fishmonger hesitated, though. "My shop is right on the docks," he said. "Of course I sell fish. What else could I sell? Hats?" He left the sign maker with his twenty dollars still in his pocket.

I was a nerdy little girl who loved word play, and the story of the thrifty fishmonger appealed to me. Then I was reminded of it, decades later, when my oldest daughter shared with me something that one of her college professors

139

had told her. She had written a three and a half page paper when the assignment was for a paper of four to six pages. She'd been a little worried that it was too short, but it was returned to her with top marks. The professor told Megan that she had a unique ability to say more than most other students, with fewer words.

This also appealed to me—the idea of writing with an economy of words.

Several years after that, I found a website called FaithWriters. I had written very little, but I was an empty nester in need of a hobby, and FaithWriters had a weekly contest for very short pieces of writing: the limit was 750 words. I used that weekly contest to hone my writing skills, and I particularly enjoyed finding ways to write interesting characters within a strict word limit.

I did pretty well in the weekly contests, and began to think of myself as a writer. Encouraged by friends and family to branch out, I thought about writing a novel—isn't that what writers are supposed to do? I gave it a month of effort, but novel writing just didn't feel right to me, and it wasn't fun. Too many words. (But I've still got a great *idea* for a novel, and it's tucked inside this book, in one of the stories here. Maybe someday …)

Lots of my writing friends were blogging, so I thought I'd try that as another outlet for my writing.

The 750-word contests demanded an economy of words—could I be even thriftier? I had to be careful; if I took that thriftiness to the same extent as the stingy fishmonger, I wouldn't write at all. But I thought it would be fun to see how much story I could cram into a few words. Maybe … just one hundred of them?

So the "100 Words" blog (now defunct; don't look for it) was born, and many of those blog posts are here, along with lots of stories that are new to this book.

I love the idea of these tiny glimpses into people's lives. In each little story, I try to choose my words carefully enough that you might be able to think, *Oh, I know her.*

ABOUT THE AUTHOR

JAN ACKERSON LIVES with her husband, Ben, in rural Michigan. A retired high school teacher, she spends her time doing occasional freelance editing and watching reality television shows.

Jan believes that learning should never stop, so in the past few years, she has worked to relearn algebra and geometry and to relearn conversational Spanish.

She enjoys spending time with her two daughters and two granddaughters, the holders of her heart.

Other interests include travel, ice cream, and most importantly, the improvement of the world through the implementation of social justice, acceptance, and expressions of grace toward all of God's children.

You can find more by Jan at her new 100 Words Stories website: https://100wordstoriessite.wordpress.com/

CPSIA information can be obtained at www.ICGtesting.com
Printed in the USA
BVOW08s1234111016

464494BV00015B/20/P